13 Cornish Ghost Stories

Foreword
Katie Fforde

I have very early memories of holidays in Cornwall. Two or maybe three families shared a farmhouse and several caravans. We played in the summer surf and tried to make sandcastles in sand that wouldn't hold together. We ate banana and jam sandwiches, pasties and bright yellow ice cream. We were always a bit cold, but we didn't care, the time whistled by. The adults piled us into the back of a huge car and took us to see churches hidden in sand dunes along narrow flower-lined lanes, ancient wishing wells, and other sights. Even as a six-year-old I realised Cornwall was a special place. We were always glad to go back another year.

Cornwall has always seemed older than the rest of the country to me. I imagine the rocks and coastline rising up from the sea before the rest of England had woken up. My childhood friends and I often played make-believe that we were Arthur and his knights living in rocky Tintagel, toughened by conflict and the search for the Holy Grail long before ordinary mortals appeared. It has always seemed on the cusp between one world and the next. There was a castle in the sea called St Michael's Mount that was rumoured to have been built by the giant Cormoran and his wife Cormelian, who dropped Chapel Rock in the middle of the causeway when her apron strings snapped. As a child I believed every word.

When I heard there was to be a book of ghost stories, I thought it was a brilliant idea. What better setting for something otherworldly could there be?

Of course, there are lots of books set in Cornwall and, as a writer, I have dipped my toe into Cornwall myself. But a selection of short stories gives the reader far more scope. It's a chance to discover new writers and, on holiday, it's fun to look for a new favourite author without having to commit to a whole novel. That said, I am certain this anthology will add authors to reading lists.

As for ghost stories, I am a firm believer in them and only a slightly less firm believer in ghosts. Of course, I don't believe in ghosts most of the time – but I find my scepticism falling away quite quickly in the right circumstances. The past is so evident in Cornwall and the division between past and present is often hardly more than a veil. I am very willing to have my disbelief suspended and read on.

There are some famous writers represented here, and some lesser known. They all have a couple of things in common. They have a deep connection with Cornwall, because they are Cornish or have lived here for a number of years, and they are all good. When you only want 13 stories you can be very particular. To be part of this anthology you have to offer your very best work. It's an honour to be included. But, for the reader, it means you are getting the jewels, the magic pathways to another world. There's something about Cornwall that makes me believe in fairies and, once you think you've caught a glimpse of a tiny person disappearing into an ancient stone wall, believing in ghosts is easy.

Perhaps you are here on holiday and want to sample some spooky Cornish tales. Or possibly you've lived here all your life and fancy dipping into some new and original stories about ghosts and things that go bump in the night. Either way, I feel there should be a copy of this book in every hotel, hostel, library, pub, and cottage. Maybe there should be a warning that this book may change how you view the supernatural, or maybe readers should just take their chance…

Introduction

Marie Macneill & Joanne Ella Parsons

When we stood together in the lunch queue at Falmouth University's Haunted Landscapes conference in 2023, we had no idea that a year later we would be editing a book of brand new stories about 13 Cornish ghosts created by writers who breathe Cornish air. It was an off the cuff idea. Followed by laughter, a pasty, and something vegetarian. The laughter was mainly because we decided we wanted to commission writers, but we didn't have any funds. However, we did (and still do) have a shared passion for the spooky, the supernatural, the scary. Stories about the dead who cannot rest until there is resolution, redemption, or restored reputation. Night-walkers, those who cannot sleep, and those who cannot rest in peace. Those who simply haunt for the sheer hell of it, and those who watch over the innocent to protect them from the evil that lies at the heart of their story.

Our next step was to ask 11 wonderful writers we knew (and approach some we didn't, through sometimes crafty means) to join us and become 13. We persuaded them to write for free with only the promise that we would try to find the right publisher. Annamaria, Emily, Emma, Graham, Jane, Kate, Liz, Nicola, Pauline, Roz, Tony – thank you for giving us your trust and your stories.

We thought Ron Johns at Mabecron Books would be the perfect Cornish publisher so asked our friend Katie Fforde to put us in touch with him. Ron immediately jumped aboard, offering his enthusiastic support for the project, and totally understood our mission to promote Cornish stories by Cornish writers. Another friend, Derek Hayes brought the ghost stories to life by creating striking illustrations.

Cornwall is the perfect setting for tales, myths, and legends. The wild moors, the granite, the clay, the rebellious sea, and flat calm coves make the county a vast and inspirational canvas. The starry nights, needle-sharp gorse, and windswept tors and carns provide perfect backdrops to eerie full moons and ghostly goings-on. Mischievous piskies dance across our landscape, while the spectres of the past, both real and imagined, haunt our memories and our dreams. There are new stories to be told around every corner, across every ley line, behind every menhir, and in the rocks and caves that litter our shores. Another 13 are already emerging from the mists.

For Chris and John
Meur ras Kernow

*To my wife Lee,
my foremost critic
and biggest champion*
Derek Hayes

Text © 2024 the contributors
Illustrations © 2024 Derek Hayes

The moral rights of the authors have been asserted.
All rights reserved.

Without limiting the rights under copyright reserved above,
no part of this publication may be reproduced, stored in or
introduced into a retrieval system, or transmitted, in any form
or by any means, without the prior permission of both copyright
owner and the publisher.

Please note that some of the stories contain strong language,
and scenes of a violent or sexual nature.

First published 2024 by Mabecron Books
Reprinted 2024

Mabecron Books Ltd
3 Briston Orchard, St Mellion, Saltash
Cornwall PL12 6RQ

Printed and bound in Great Britain by Clays Ltd

ISBN 978-1-73-986133-9

13 CORNISH GHOST STORIES

Edited by
Marie Macneill *and* **Joanne Ella Parsons**

Illustrated by
Derek Hayes

M
Mabecron Books

The Stories

The Blind Spots • *Kate Riordan*	10
Annie's Ghost • *Marie Macneill*	28
The Ghost of Dozmary Pool • *Roz Watkins*	48
The Black Zawn • *Jane Johnson*	64
The Todden • *Emma Cowell*	80
The Drummer Boy • *Liz Fenwick*	96
The Storm Bells • *Pauline Sheppard*	112
Celia • *Graham Mitchell*	120
The Blow In • *Joanne Ella Parsons*	136
Till Death Do Us Part • *Tony Cowell*	148
The Trouble with Being Dead • *Emily Barr*	160
Treloyhan Manor • *Nicola K Smith*	180
The Visitors • *Annamaria Murphy*	204

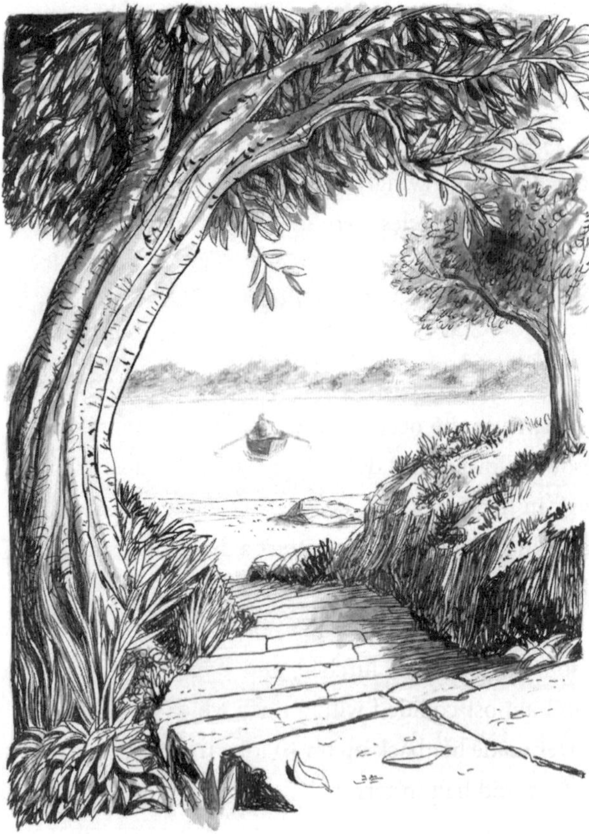

The Blind Spots
Kate Riordan

The lane was unnervingly narrow and seemed to be getting worse. Her neck muscles were starting to protest, so tightly was she gripping the steering wheel. The listing on the holiday rental site had said Fowey, she was sure of it, but this was patently not Fowey.

She had a strong suspicion that the town was on the other side of the river she occasionally caught a glimpse of when the hedgerows allowed it: a dull silver ribbon because the day was overcast. In her memories, decades old now, the skies here had been a faultless blue, the river waters a deep mysterious jade that hadn't seemed entirely English, somehow.

Her low-slung car, its suspension designed for motorways and suburban avenues, lurched and creaked around another bend and almost collided with a dirty white van going too fast. The driver made her back up for so long that she began to shake, half in fury and half in terror that she would simply shut down, unable to master the coordination to reverse any further.

Finally he roared past, leaving her and the car so thoroughly wedged into the hedgerow that the paintwork would be scratched. *What a dickhead*, she said under her breath as she moved off again. It felt good so she said it again, much louder this time, hysteria swelling inside her.

She wished she could tell Eddie about it. She was good at anecdotes. He would have laughed, especially when she got to the dickhead bit. She wished she could tell him so badly that it formed a mass in her throat that she couldn't swallow down. What was that philosophical question about a tree falling in the forest? Something about it not making any sound if no one was there to hear it. She wondered if widowhood was turning her into that theoretical tree, telling a dead man silly stories about her day.

The lane wound on, tipping ever more steeply downward, the hawthorn flanking the car so tall and dense now that there were no more flashes of river. The turning for the house came at the very instant she was about to give up the whole thing as a mistake, or perhaps even a scam – you did hear about these things. But there it was: a dark wooden plaque with elegant gold lettering, lit by a stray dart of sun.

She parked in a gravelled area behind the house which was almost level with the pitched grey roof because the plot dropped so steeply to the water below. Built to face the view, it wasn't a very large house, but it sprawled to compensate for the gradient. Oaks, beeches, and enormous glossy-leaved shrubs pressed in around it, and the steps she went down in search of the front door were slick with moss. A line from a poem came to her then, from nowhere. *Houses put on leaves. Water rang.* Here was a place that nature would take back swiftly, if it was permitted.

When she closed the door behind her, the house seemed to exhale and then settle again, like a creature roused and now sinking back into sleep. She took in the faded rugs woven in shades of rose and mist, and the gleam of the hall's soft-worn flags. It was beautiful. No, more than that. It was *enchanting*, a word stolen from a fairy tale. Of course, it would have been prohibitively expensive if it had been on the outskirts of Fowey. She saw that now.

She'd been right about the river, though. There was an old map framed in the hallway, an ornate black cross marking the house with Fowey on the other side, tucked away around a bend. In a boat it would probably take no more than ten minutes. By road it would be at least half an hour, all the way back up to Lerryn and round along more of those perilous lanes.

Her breathing was loud in the great silence of the house. She still hadn't got used to being alone; she could count on one hand the nights she'd spent apart from Eddie during their marriage. Suddenly, it seemed quite mad what she had done: coming to this place on the strength of a dream she'd had not long after the funeral.

In fact, it had been as much memory as dream, drawn as it was from a week the two of them had spent in Fowey during the heatwave summer of '76. The town was choked with holidaymakers and Eddie had the bright idea of hiring a rowing boat. It was such a relief out there on the water; the tree-lined banks retaining a cool lushness when everywhere else felt parched and grubby. In the dream, she had trailed her fingers in the water while he rowed them upriver in his rolled-up shirtsleeves, damp cotton moving over shoulder muscle as he pulled the oars through the water, fat jewels of it scattering as he lifted the blades clear.

When she couldn't shake the dream – didn't want to be rid of it, anyway – she went online and this was the first house that had come up. She hadn't hesitated.

Now, the reality of the situation beginning to crowd her thoughts, she made herself take some deep breaths, four counts in and six out. She had to do this quite often now, since Eddie. If she concentrated hard enough, it had the power to halt the panic that otherwise began crawling hotly up her spine.

When she felt more like herself, she thought she ought to inspect the house. It was strikingly lovely, though its hotch-potch of styles and eras shouldn't have worked as harmoniously as they did. The hall looked to be very old indeed, with walls two feet thick and undulating plaster that caught and held the shadows. Further on, and into a generous sitting room, the place passed into its Georgian period, with book-lined alcoves and tall sash windows through which the gentle light of late afternoon fell.

Yes, it was very beautiful. It was just... Well, it was just that there was such *heft* to the silence, somehow, as though the air weighed more than it usually did. She knew she was skirting round what she really thought – that the house didn't feel quite empty.

Before that notion took proper hold, she retraced her steps back to find the newly done kitchen she'd admired on the website. It was even higher-spec than she remembered, and all that expensive chrome – American-style fridge, designer extractor fan, the polished dials of a huge range she probably wouldn't use – was a comfort.

She would be fine here. She was tempted to say it aloud. *I will be fine here.* But, unlike in the car, she didn't quite have the nerve. Well, it was only three days. She would read and go for walks. There was a car ferry somewhere on this side, she recalled, and a pub teetering just above the road where the cars queued to get over to Fowey. It had river views at the front for the tourists and a dimly lit bar at the back for locals. It was right next to the du Maurier house, with its cheery, blue-painted windows.

But another internal voice piped up then, and it was her child-self, fearful of everything, who still rose to the surface sometimes, at unhelpful moments. *Wait till it gets dark*, it said.

'Oh, do shut up,' she said, daring to speak aloud this time.

She had been right to be wary, though. Her voice was too much in the expectant house – even in that sparkling new kitchen. It recoiled from her, bristling with reproach. She knew then that no one had spoken in the house for a long, long time.

After an hour, she still hadn't ventured upstairs. She should just get it over with: choose one of the bedrooms, unpack her things, change her shoes for her slippers. Mundane tasks anywhere else, here they were beginning to feel like things she was actively avoiding. She knew why, too, and it was another instinct that seemed more animal than reasonable. It was because going upstairs would take her more deeply into the house's strange embrace. She was afraid she would feel it physically tighten around her.

Instead, she drifted towards the bifold doors at the far end of the kitchen. On the other side of them, a smooth lawn rolled out towards the slow shifting surface of what was really more creek than river. It really was beautiful here, she reassured herself again. If only it wasn't so... But she stopped that thought.

She wrestled with the doors, the mechanism too minimalist to offer any clues until it suddenly clicked and the enormous panes slid away from her like they weighed nothing. She didn't notice immediately, so relieved to have got them open at all, but the air outside felt just the same as it did inside. It wasn't so much the temperature, though it was very mild for late September. It was that it didn't move. She sucked a sharp breath in, certain for an odd little moment that there was no air left, like on the surface of the moon. That everything had simply stopped, time held fast, the normal rules dissolved.

Real unease crept in with the dusk, as she had known it would. What she needed was a bit of inane noise to drown out the house's silent murmurs. The television crouched on top of the sitting room mantel, an incongruously huge blank eye in the space where a soothing landscape should have hung. She couldn't get it to come on, and the frustration of it made her tearful because she was actually quite handy with gadgets. It was she who had tuned things in and set things up when they were bought. Eddie had always been hopeless – jabbing at buttons and making it worse – so it seemed especially unfair.

She went back to the kitchen to try the radio she'd seen there instead: a handsome retro thing the colour of a robin's egg. This at least turned on, but there was nothing but static.

Actually, that wasn't true. As she inched the dial along the wavebands, she caught distant voices and, once, a brief snatch of music, something she hadn't heard for many years, old-fashioned and melancholy, and which had gone again before she could quite grasp it.

She was about to give up when a low whisper came through, making her freeze.

Wait for us, she thought it said, the sibilance of the *us* a soft hiss.

It came again then, slightly louder and deeper this time, and the air around her quivered in response. She fumbled in her rush to turn the dial back off, breathing loud and ragged in the abrupt quiet. To be absolutely sure, she traced the power cable towards the socket further along the wall, intending to pull out the plug but finding it already done. *Batteries*, Eddie said in her head, clear as day. *There'll be batteries in the back.*

It was just the sort of sensible thing he might've said. She didn't check, though. Because what if there weren't any?

A bottle of red wine had been left for her on the kitchen island's stone top, along with some biscuits and a foil packet of teabags. She made herself think about the cleaner who must have left them there for her, and her blood slowed a little. She would open the wine now, she decided, though she hadn't had a drop since the funeral. It would take the edge off.

After the first glass, drunk down quickly at the worktop, she felt calmer. Slightly detached from proceedings, which was exactly what she was after. She poured another and let herself be lured back to the bifold doors. This time she got the hang of them immediately, pushing them as far back as they went so there was no chance they would slide back and lock her out.

While the house rested cool and damp in its caul of greenery, the lawn had evidently spent the summer in full sun. It had been one of the driest since the famous one, when she was here before. At the garden's extent was a low wooden fence with a small wicket gate. From there, a steep flight of stone steps went down to the grey mudflats that edged the water.

The light was almost gone from the day now, little left of it but a wavering band of primrose yellow in the west, squeezed between heavy stripes of cloud. At home, the streetlights would be coming on, the squat front-room lamps of her neighbours. Here, there was nothing but the thickening shadows in the steep-sided woods and the soft sheen of the creek. A bird's cry echoed across the banks, totally unlike the plump warble of the wood pigeons she associated with twilight. This sounded wild, prehistoric.

She turned to study the house, to see if she could understand its shape and form better from a different angle, but all she could absorb were the dark empty sockets of the windows. Hadn't she turned on the spotlights in the kitchen, and the light in the hall? She wasn't sure now – the wine had gone to her head. Well, good. She would get some more.

She was halfway back across the lawn, planting her feet carefully, when the bifold doors began to move. She caught their movement in her peripheral vision and, for a split-second, she didn't believe it and stopped, blinking, to clear her vision. But it was true. Slowly, silently, they were gliding shut. It was like her earlier precaution had given them the idea.

She dropped her glass and ran, getting there faster than she would have thought possible, easily catching the doors in time. Still, she was breathing hard as she stepped inside and pulled them closed behind her. *They must be on a slope*, she willed Eddie to say in her head – or else something about subsidence, because of the house's proximity to the water. But he remained stubbornly quiet. It was never his voice at all, she thought, to be cruel to herself. Only mine. He'll never say anything again. She bent over, winded by the terrible truth of it.

By the time the wine was finished, she was drunk as she hadn't been in years. There was no way she'd be able to drive now if she needed to leave. She hadn't thought of that when she opened the bottle.

Heading upstairs, finally, she was off kilter, misjudging the turn halfway up and banging into the wall hard enough that she knew a bruise would mark her friable old skin. It didn't really hurt but another wave of despair went through her which suddenly twisted into anger, the first she'd really felt towards him. *You won't ever leave me, will you?* It was an old refrain of hers, nearly as old as their marriage. *Course not*, he'd always said. And later added, when they were getting old, *You first, and me right behind.*

'Where are you?' she couldn't help but say now, to the empty bedroom. The air shimmered. The clothes she'd automatically arranged so they only took up half the wardrobe's rail swayed slightly, but it wasn't him doing it, she knew. It wouldn't ever be him again.

With the day gone and the television still unresponsive, she took her comfort in books, just as she had as a child, afraid to lie there in the dark once her parents had gone to bed. In the sitting room, there were three whole shelves devoted to Cornwall, a mixture of fiction and biography and dog-eared Ordnance Survey maps. Arthur Quiller-Couch was there, and what looked to be a full roster of du Mauriers, the short story collections as well as the novels. She hesitated over *Rebecca* and *Frenchman's Creek*, old friends, read so many times that their power to unnerve had long since faded, but would probably re-emerge here. Non-fiction would be safer.

In the high four-poster bed, propped up against the pillows, she tried to lose herself in local tales: the skirmishes of the Fowey Gallants, and the great iron chain that had been raised across the harbour mouth, sixteen inches thick, whenever the Spanish and Dutch fleets materialised out of a moonless night. The secret gathering of American troops in 1944, before they crossed the sea to face the enemy at Omaha Beach. She read of Dungarth, the last king of ancient Cornwall, drowned upriver by the pitiless Saxons.

She woke with a pounding heart a few hours later, still sitting up with a book in her lap but the bedside lamp now switched off, when she knew for certain she'd left it on.

It took her a beat to realise that it wasn't just the wine making her blood pound, but a noise she couldn't make sense of. In fact, the low rumbling was as much sensation as sound, reverberating through the floors and her own solar plexus. She sat up straight, eyes straining in the dark because she couldn't find the lamp's switch, until the lightless air began to swirl and eddy around her like waves. Panicked, she swung her legs out of the bed and stumbled towards the windows, yanking back the wooden shutters.

Tangled in skeins of high cloud was a new moon, only just bright and brave enough to illuminate the creek below. She tugged at the window catch because it was suddenly imperative that she identified the sound before it was lost. When she'd got it open, she leant right out, holding her breath to hear better, and the answer came to her in a glorious rush.

It was a train. Just a train.

Now she knew, the realisation wonderfully benign, she could clearly hear the rhythm of it passing over sleepers somewhere on the opposite bank, a heavy clackety-clack, clackety-clack. And then it must have reached a point where the trees thinned because suddenly she could see it, too: the long, lit-up carriages like flickering beacons; a pall of smoke rising to meet the sky, grey against deepest blue.

It was so late for a train to be running, though, wasn't it? Too late? The thought hovered darkly over her and she made herself picture the driver who must be out there, just across the water. An ordinary man, still bleary with sleep, unscrewing the cap on his thermos. And then, even better, a new realisation came: it must be a freight train. The lights she'd seen weren't from inside carriages. They were sparks from the rails where the wheels ground against them, forged from the weight of carrying their heavy loads through the night.

Calm now, she left the window wide and returned to bed, falling instantly into untroubled sleep.

She woke late – far later than she ever did at home. She'd had the dream again – the very one that brought her here: Eddie and her in the little rowing boat, young again. When she got out of bed, her balance was peculiar, as though she'd spent the whole night out on the water.

She took her morning cup of tea outside, shading her eyes because yesterday's cloud had slunk away in the night, leaving the creek gleaming under a bright sun. There was a swing-seat by the wooden fence she hadn't seen yesterday – how had she missed it? It was just like the one her parents had had in the garden of the house where she grew up. Someone had positioned it so it looked not downriver towards Fowey but up, to where the water diverged and became two narrower creeks that snaked out of sight. On the spit of land that bisected them stood a lone heron, which remained still for so long that she thought her eyes must be playing tricks. But then it lifted away, the flap of its huge wings so unhurried as to make flight seem miraculous.

She had no urge to go to Fowey today. None at all. She swung gently, rocking on her heels to keep the seat swinging, and had almost drifted off again when the certainty that someone was in the garden made her rear up clumsily; the seat's chains clanking as she took in the slight figure standing there as motionless as the heron, oddly colourless against the vivid tones of the day.

Fear gripped her so quickly and completely that she thought she would fall down, but then the figure raised a hand and stepped towards her.

'I've made 'ee startle,' he called out, because it was a man, she saw now – an ancient fleshless man whose face had that collapsed look seen in old photographs, from a time when it was commonplace for people to lose their teeth. He approached, smiling, and she did the same until they met in the dead-centre of the lawn. His eyes, she saw now, were bird-bright and alert, and so ink-black that there was no distinguishing between iris and pupil. 'I'm sorry, maid. I pass this way most days as a shortcut.' He gestured towards the steps that ran down to the narrow beach.

She laughed, not least because he'd called her maid, which she was surely half a century too old for. 'Please don't apologise. I was dozing, that's all.'

'Dint sleep well?' He cocked his head, looking even more bird-like.

'Oh no, I did. Although… Well, I did wake in the night. It was the train. I didn't know there was a line here, but then I realised it must be freight, which was why it was running so late. It occurred to me this morning that it was probably something to do with the china clay…' She ground to a halt at his quizzical expression. 'There's a china clay…' – she didn't know what to call it: factory? Plant? – 'isn't there? Somewhere round here? I remember seeing it when we – my husband and I, my late husband – took a boat out on the water, many years ago now.'

'Certainly there is,' he said. 'That way, round the bend. White gold, they called it. Best stuff in the world. You might see a boat heading out. Big flat things they are, can't miss 'em. Trains, though? No. The last of them ran last year. Line's all grown over. And the passenger service hasn't run since the sixties. Not since Beeching come along with his axe.'

The noise came back to her then – its intimation of enormous weight. The flickering lights and engine smoke she knew she hadn't dreamt either.

The fear stole back in swiftly, ice-water sluicing through her. 'But I heard it,' she said stupidly. 'I saw it.'

'Some do,' he said, nodding. 'Not everyone, but some.'

She gaped at him, unable to say more.

He moved towards the steps, passing close enough that she smelled him. Wood-smoke, sugary tea, and Pears soap. She knew that combination, an old scent that must have been waiting quietly inside her since she was tiny. A wide lap, hands holding her steady, gold rings on swollen fingers. The fear ebbed a little.

'You seen anything else?' he said, turning back.

'What do you mean?' She knew she should make a joke, retrieve her cup and bustle back to the house before she heard anything she couldn't unhear. Words that would accompany her through the day and into darkening evening. But she waited as he considered. Behind him, the creek winked and glinted at her.

'Some see them in the gloaming,' he said eventually. 'If you're that way inclined. Low sun in winter is another time. It happens when the light is thrown queer. They likes hiding in the blind spots, I s'pose.'

'Who?' she said, hardly more than a whisper, 'Who do you mean?'

But he hadn't heard her. He'd already turned, hand raised in farewell, closing the little wicket gate behind him.

She went to it, half expecting, half dreading that there would be no sign of him. That he would have vanished into the lemon-coloured morning like vapour. But there he was, his stance alert as though he was searching for something further up the flat, beyond the seams of driftwood and bladderwrack.

And then she saw what it was. A dog, rangy and reddish in the sunshine, running at full pelt towards him. She watched as the man stopped and bent, spreading his arms wide in greeting.

She went down there after they'd disappeared out of sight, not wanting to intrude. Small white clouds had appeared in the sky, scudding along fast in a wind much too high to be felt on the ground. They covered and uncovered the sun so that shadows came and went again, the light flattening and then splitting, flattening and splitting. *When the light is thrown queer*, she thought.

She could see the man's footprints clearly in the damp mud. She could see exactly where he'd stopped to greet his dog. But there were no paw prints, not a single one. She went further along, bending down to look more closely. The dog was too light and fast to make any indentation, she told herself, though she knew, really, that this wasn't true. Knew why the man came every day to see his dog; why the dog wasn't with him already. She knew. And it made something light and luminous swoop inside her. It took her a moment to understand that it wasn't fear – that it was closer to its opposite.

Hope.

She dressed for the dusk, for the gloaming, without quite realising she had. She'd not bothered with make-up since losing Eddie. What was the point? But she enjoyed the old rhythms of it now; the performance at the dressing table, the caretaking of her own body. She put her hair up as she hadn't in years, her fingers remembering what to do. It seemed as though her hair did, too, waving back from her face in the right way, submitting easily to the pins.

When she finished, she peered at herself and saw that she was quite transformed. The mirror's foxed, she told herself. *I'm* foxed, here, in this house. But as she rose from the little velvet stool, her body felt… Well, she could hardly feel it at all, that was the point. Nothing internally pulled or ached. Nothing hurt.

As she went down the stairs, pictures spun and glimmered in her mind. Faces of people she didn't know, but who had been here before her. She grasped the smooth wood of the bannister and it was already warm. Behind the closed door of the sitting room, she heard something like whispers, but she wasn't certain until a peal of laughter rang out, just for a second before it was hushed.

The wicket gate was open when she reached it. She took the steps carefully out of habit, though she could have run down them without mishap. The light was strange and lovely now, the pale mud turned lavender by the rosy sky. Light welled inside her, and not just in the sense of brightness. There was a weightlessness inside her, too. It floated in her chest like a golden bubble.

Waiting there on the soft mud, her mind returned to that afternoon in the rowing boat, and how she'd told Eddie that it was on the same stretch of water that Daphne du Maurier first saw Boy Browning. She'd been out there with her sister in a little boat like theirs and saw this handsome man sailing his own vessel with ease. There and then, she'd fallen in love with him.

Eddie had smiled and nodded while she told him. He liked how she collected little facts and stories, magpie-like. He admired her bookish side because he wasn't like that at all; they were clever in different ways. Much later, she'd read a biography of du Maurier and discovered that she'd often been unhappy in her marriage, that Browning had affairs she found out about, and that she spent much of her time alone. That wasn't how *her* life with Eddie had turned out at all. She'd been lucky like that, they both had.

As with the train, sound came to her long before she saw anything. The syrupy plash of the disturbed water, the muffled clank of the oarlocks as they turned. She waited there in the fading light, eyes trained on the creek that perfectly reflected the sky. Trained on the places where the current's slow roil made flashes and sparks out of the dying light. She watched them carefully, the blind spots from where she knew he'd soon emerge, having not gone without her at all, just as he had always promised he wouldn't.

Author's Note

The lines of poetry quoted are from 'Healing a Lunatic Boy' by Charles Causley (*Collected Poems 1951–1975*, Macmillan London Limited, 1975).

Annie's Ghost

Marie Macneill

Lauren wasn't interested. She did not have time for all this hoo-ha nonsense and, when another bar bore started up about Annie George's antics, she was hard pushed not to tut her annoyance. She folded indignant arms and thought about how she was literally trapped behind a polished mahogany bar and brass beer pumps.

Serving customers? Who would have thought it? Entertaining the locals while they droned on about things that 'go bump in the night'. Upstairs. In this actual pub.

Up where Lauren and Simon were so tired that very little had gone bump since they arrived – especially at night! And no, no, she hadn't seen or heard Annie's ghost. Not once. Not so much as shadow or footstep.

Although, it had to be said, neither she nor Simon were keen on going into Annie's room. After a quick peek on the day they arrived, the bedroom door had remained firmly closed. Sensibility told Lauren that there was nothing malevolent in there, yet she still shivered as a miasmic memory assaulted her nostrils in the seconds between the door being opened and shut. She had glimpsed the iron-framed bed, with its ornate wrought head and footboard, and the puffed-up, paisley-patterned eiderdown. A brass-handled, dark oak, wardrobe and matching chest of drawers. A worn Afghan rug run across tar-stained floorboards. A small, framed, pen and ink picture of the First and Last public house in the 1800s, when it truly was the first and last building in Cornwall. And finally, on the wall next to it a faded print of Sennen Sands, where Annie had taken her last breath and swallowed up the sea. Annie was laid out in this small square room before being buried, 'without pomp or circumstance', in an unmarked grave beyond the sanctuary of the church next door and its consecrated ground.

'Your last lot just upped and went,' said Two-Fingers. Presumably named because of his way of telling folk to 'stick it'. Most especially after consuming a jar or two. She sighed inwardly, realising how much she was already infected by the local lingo.

A jar or two? Really? How very Penwith. Next up, I'll be buying into the idea that the pub is actually haunted, and women and rabbits are not allowed in fishermen's boats!

'Is this the same old yarn you told me yesterday?' she asked.

Two-Fingers pouted.

'Okay then,' she said, swallowing the grump that was rising in her throat. 'Go on, tell me, what happened to make the previous tenants up and leave.'

'Their cat was shut in the wardrobe. Three nights in a row. It was Annie. No question.' Two-Fingers splayed his hands to punctuate his statement. An unlit rollie dancing between his index and middle finger.

'Annie did it.'

'Annie the ghost?'

''Zackly.'

'200 years-old-plus and still on her feet?'

Two-Fingers nodded, putting the unlit rollie to his mouth, and taking it out again.

'Whatever she took, I'll have some. I'm hard pushed to stand upright after two hours of serving you lot.' Lauren's laugh lacked warmth.

On the bar stool next to Two-Fingers, Bob-Job wheezed, 'No need to get personal there.'

'I'm not. And I'm probably not nearly personal enough for this trade either, am I?'

'Your words, not mine,' said Two-Fingers, carefully putting his thin-stick cigarette back into his tobacco tin. Lauren noticed the 15 golden bezants hand-painted on the lid. The tin itself, old and rusty.

Simon, catching the tail of the conversation from the other end of the bar, threw Lauren a look. That look. Lauren stared back, fronting it out. She didn't like the way he seemed to disapprove. It was not her idea to come to the arse-end of the UK, live in a draughty pub and entertain barflies in the deadbeat afternoon. And come summer, it would be worse, they'd be knee-deep in scampi, Chardonnay, and chips. She had thought that being here would mean wild walks along the clifftops, frolics in frothy waves, and sandy Sundays on the beach. On arrival, she discovered that there was no time for anything other than prep, serving, clearing, and the now not-infrequent quarrelling with Simon. The supplement magazine cliché that had inspired their post-pandemic journey from London to Cornwall had quickly evaporated into coastal fog, grey mizzle, and downpour rain that played across most of their daily skies.

'Was it the pub cat?' asked Simon, moving into the conversation.

Two-Fingers stroked his straggly goatee. 'Well, yes.'

'You don't have a cat, do you?' asked Bob-Job.

'Do we look like cat people?' Lauren barked indignantly.

'It was a proper mouser. Used to leave them on the flagstones.' Two-Fingers pointed towards the inglenook. 'Over there, in front of the fire. Then one night it caught a rat. And that's when it all started. Same night, after lights out, Jen, the landlady before you, heard the cat mewing. Couldn't find her at first. Annie's door was always closed see, and no one would have thought of looking in there. Jen wandered down the stairs. Couldn't find nothing. The mewing had stopped by this time. So she went back to bed. Which was next to Annie's room. The mewing started up again. She got up again, but this time she went into the room. Nothing. Then a mew, and it sounded like it was coming from inside the wardrobe. She opened the door, and found the cat was cowering in the corner. Despite the wardrobe door and the bedroom door being shut tight. How on earth did it get in? Some kind of black magic. Most folk round here reckoned it was Annie.'

'Come back to explain her position,' added Bob-Job.

'Meaning?' asked Simon.

'Meaning, Dionysius Williams,' Two-Fingers replied.

'Who?' asked Simon.

'Annie's landlord.'

'With a name like that, he would have to be, wouldn't he? Hah, Dionysius!' said Lauren.

'No. That's not it at all. She rented the pub from him. That kind of landlord. She was the landlady of the pub. The tenant, just like you. And he was her landlord. But the thing was, she didn't pay him no rent. It was an understanding see, except after a time he started getting teasy about it.'

'Or greedy,' chipped in Bob-Job.

'Or greedy. And she, knowing things she shouldn't have known, used it to her advantage,' said Two-Fingers, fixing Lauren with his gimlet eyes.

'What's all this got to with a cat catching a rat?' said Lauren, a little uncomfortable at being pinned by Two-Fingers' piercing stare.

'You haven't heard all this before?' said Two-Fingers.

'Not from you,' said Simon.

'Oh, please,' said Lauren, wringing the tea towel in her hands.

Two-Fingers matched Lauren's frown with a smile. 'He was a smuggler – a lot of it about in them days. Free rent bought him Annie's silence. Mind you, she was in on a lot of it too. There's a secret passage that do run under the floor here and do go all the way down to the beach. They had some kind of fall out. He wanted Annie out. But it was her livelihood and her kingdom. She weren't going no place. Things got nasty. Annie turned King's evidence and Dionysius went to gaol. The smugglers down Sennen Cove…' Two-Fingers splayed his hands again '…were not happy, to say the least. No one was.'

Lauren rolled her eyes. 'Ancient history. What's all that got to do with some curious cat in a wardrobe? I expect next you'll tell me it was a black cat. What a load of cobblers.'

'You're right, it was a black cat. And the very next night, it was found in Annie's wardrobe again. No one could work out how it got there and how it got through them two doors. Then on the third night something spooked the landlady...'

'Jen?' In spite of herself, Lauren was listening wide-eyed.

'Jen,' said Two-Fingers.

'Big time,' said Bob-Job, nodding.

'And she left. Never to return. Last seen heading for Penzance,' concluded Two-Fingers, theatrically slapping his thighs with the palms of his hands.

'What about her husband?' Lauren eyes widened further.

'He was driving her. Both petrified from what we heard,' said Two-Fingers.

'Thass it,' added Bob-Job, solemn-faced.

Two-Fingers picked up his glass, downed the contents and jumped off his bar stool. 'Right, that's me. Work ain't going to do itself. See you dreckly. Coming Bob-Job?'

'Right on,' said Bob-Job.

Lauren watch the two men leave and turned to Simon. 'And?'

'And I guess we'll have to wait for the next exciting instalment.'

'Dreckly?' Lauren sniffed.

'At a guess. C'mon, honey,' Simon said, patting Lauren's arm and giving her a consolatory smile. 'It could be worse.'

'Could it?'

Lauren was standing outside an outhouse when she saw Sheila coming towards her. 'I thought you went home hours ago,' she said.

'I did. But I had to come back to feed her. What you doing of out here?'

'Simon's covering for me. He told me I needed some fresh air. I told him I needed a fresh life.' Lauren shrugged off a sigh. 'I am so tired. But I am so grateful for you. If you weren't here I would be doing all the cleaning on top of everything else. Feed who?'

'Come see.'

Sheila pushed open the stable-style door and put her finger to her lips. Lauren peered around the granite and cob wall. In a corner, on top of a bed of straw, was a little black kitten. Mewing. Looking at Lauren and Sheila through sleepy pale eyes.

'Who's is it?' asked Lauren.

'Yours?' said Sheila.

'I have a hard enough job looking after myself.'

Sheila crouched down and tickled the kitten under the chin. 'Cute or what?'

Lauren held out her hand until she could feel the kitten's warm breath on her fingertips. The kitten purred. Lauren yielded and purred back. 'And where did you come from?'

'I found her.'

'Is she a she?'

'I think so. I found her in the car park. By the old church wall.'

'Dumped?'

'Who knows? I brought her in here. I knew there was straw left over from stuffing Guy Fawkes.'

'What do you think?'

'I don't.'

'Every pub needs a cat.'

Sheila looked into Lauren's eyes.

Lauren looked back. 'You can be very persuasive.'

'Can I?'

'Yes.' Lauren cleared her throat. 'Maybe we'll keep her for a little while. Just until we find out where she belongs.'

Lauren was drowning.

Sand and grit filling her mouth and nostrils. Foaming salt waves stinging her eyeballs. Screams and yells for help snatched away by the wicked wind. Swallowing salty water, spitting, coughing, gagging. The crash and roar of the sea drumming her ears. A pressure on her shoulder. Something shaking her side. Simon gently shushing her, 'You're dreaming, honey. It's just a bad dream. Shush now. Shush.'

'Sorry, I'm sorry,' she mumbled.

'No, don't be, it's fine, it's okay, you're safe.'

Awake now, she turned and put her hand on Simon's shoulder. 'Thank you. Sorry. I was shouting for help, but nothing was coming out of my mouth. It was like I'd been gagged, and I was drowning, in the sea, and no one could save me. Oh my God, it was horrible.'

'You sounded like the little kitten. Mewing.'

Lauren sat bolt upright and fumbled for the switch on the bedside lamp and turned on the light. She leapt across the bed and looked into the corner of the room where she had placed a box and blanket for the kitten. It was empty. 'Where is she?'

Simon joined her at the end of the bed. 'I've no idea.'

Lauren grabbed her phone and turned on its torchlight, swung herself over the bed, and looked under it.

'Is she there?' asked Simon.

'No.'

And then they heard it.

A mew. Mewing. But where from?

'That's what you sounded like.'

'What?'

'When you were having that bad dream.'

'No, I was screaming for help.'

'Yes I know, but you sounded like that. Listen.'

A plaintive mew-mew filled the silence in the room.

'But the door is shut. She can't have got out. She must still be in here.'

'It doesn't sound like it's coming from in here. I think it's coming from next door.'

'Annie's room?' Lauren shivered.

'Want me to go check? Hey, come on, it's just an empty room.'

'Yes, yes please.' She felt feeble and a little afraid but consoled herself by reasoning that she was still perturbed by her nightmare.

'Are you okay? You're not scared, are you?' Simon asked.

'Course not,' she replied with a brisk lie. 'I just want to know how the kitten got out. That's all.'

'Maybe it slipped out before we shut the door properly?'

'Maybe.' Lauren wasn't convinced.

'Hey, it's a very old, creaky, creepy, crooked pub. Tunnels, hidey holes…'

'What are you suggesting?'

'Nothing. Except there'll be some rational explanation.'

Alone, Lauren tried to calm herself by breathing. In-two-three, out-two-three, in-two-three, out-two-three. Goosebumps raced across her arms, up the back of her neck, and as a clammy fear claimed her forehead, she felt an icy hand touch her cheek.

She shrieked. Her breath shallow and panting. 'Simon?'

Instead of opening her eyes to see, she squeezed them tighter still. Scared of what it might be, her hand flew to her cheek and grasped at… nothing. Air. Nothing there. Her fingers flailed, attempting to touch something solid. Nothing.

She stuttered, confronting her fear, 'Just try… and be… not like this… you're upset. You've had a bad dream, that's all. Simon will be back any second with the kitten. And all will be well.'

The door flew open. She gasped. Simon was standing in the jamb, bearing the kitten like a gift. 'You're not going to believe this.'

'What?'

'It was in the wardrobe… and…'

Lauren cut in, '… the door was shut.'

'The snitching didn't stop with Dionysius. Next up was Christopher Pollard, he wasn't local, he was from Madron. He got off, mind. Being a Madron boy probably made all the difference. Then there was the Vingoe family, now they were local, and finally Annie's husband's brother, John George.'

'But was it Annie though?' asked Bob-Job.

Two-Fingers tapped his tobacco tin with his finger and continued. 'Well they did fall out. Over some tobacco deal. He was hanged. Sennen folk had had enough. But indeed, was it Annie who told the revenue men the tale?'

Bob-Job's eyes lit up. 'There was hell to pay.'

Lauren watched as the kitten wandered into the bar, thinking, Annie George was a cheat, a whistle-blower, a con artist, a disloyal smuggler, and an old woman. She ran a pub, had her fingers in the coastline's contraband pies, and ran a lucrative racket from shipwreck to shore. But why would Annie snitch on her crew? Why would she dob in the hands that fed her? Why cut off her nose to spite her face?'

Lauren noticed a shadow fall across the door between the public bar and the private quarters. 'Is that you, Sheila?'

'Yes, I'm off now. I'll order some more toilet paper for the Ladies before I go.' Sheila came into the room and spying the kitten under a nearby table, she bent down and stroked her head. The kitten mewed. 'She's in a long line, I reckon.'

'A long line?' asked Lauren.

'Yes, I think so. She has Sennen cat features, don't you think?'

'What, two eyes, four legs, and a tail?'

'Look more closely, Lauren.'

Lauren peered at the kitten. It looked a black, blue-eyed, bundle of fluff. Everything was in proportion. There was nothing to show that she was different to any other cat. What on earth did Sheila mean by Sennen cat features? This was all beginning to sound like folk horror.

'Where did she come from, Sheila?'

'I told you, I found her in the car park. Abandoned, probably.'

'And how did she end up in Annie's wardrobe last night?'

'I don't know. I wasn't there.'

'What do you know?'

'About Annie?'

'Yes.'

'She didn't deserve to die like that.'

'Like what?'

'The tide was full out when they pegged her down on the sands. There was no escaping, but to make sure they covered her with fish netting. Left her there, howling like the wind. And as the incoming tide rose up, so she drowned. A horrible way to pay. Especially when it was born out of misunderstanding.'

Lauren looked at Sheila in shock. 'Oh my God. That's awful. How could they? Oh my God, no wait. I dreamt I was drowning. Last night. I felt a hand on my shoulder. I was…'

'The kitten is a sign of good fortune.'

'For whom?'

'For Annie. You have been chosen. She has chosen you. The kitten is a gift.'

'To what end?'

'Annie seeks salvation. She is tired. She needs eternal rest. But she cannot rest until the world knows the truth.'

'I'm not getting this. What truth? How do you know all of this? And if you know, why can't you tell it? Chosen? Come on Sheila, this like happened hundreds of years ago.'

'I've work to do now,' said Sheila, striding away.

'Sheila?' Lauren called after her. Sheila did not look back.

Lauren looked down at the kitten, picked it up, and stroked the top of its head. 'Come on you, and no more hiding in the wardrobe when we get in.' Lauren shook her head in disbelief. 'No, it's all absolute nonsense. You're a kitten. I don't normally like cats, but you're kind of cute. You might be a Sennen cat, but you are not Annie's ghost.'

'It'll be fun, said Simon. 'Bob-Job, Two-Fingers, and Sheila have all said it'll be the best way to clear the air.'

'A séance? After what happened last night?'

'Aw, come on, you were overwrought. You had this dream thing and then your brain fried for a bit. We're stressed. This is all new to us. This pub venture thing. Really, it is. But a séance?

Could be a dream ticket, you know? A bit of weird ghostly events and the tourists and locals will flock in here. Drinking our drink, spending their money, and we're living in clover. What do you say? Is it a yes for the Ouija board?'

'No. Like no. Flat no. It'd be a con. And we'd be messing with Annie and maybe she wouldn't like that.'

When she thought about it afterwards, Lauren could not pinpoint why she looked towards the bar at that particular moment and how she knew that the glass, which was by no means on the edge of the shelf, would smash to the flagstone floor and splinter into a hundred glittering fragments. Was Annie there? Listening? Forcing Lauren to agree to the séance so she could get in touch? No, that was beyond ridiculous.

'Can you hear your actual self?' Simon's words were drowned out by the exploding glass. He leapt across to inspect the damage, looked up at the shelf, nonplussed. 'What the hell…?'

'Okay, let's do it,' said Lauren, heading behind the bar and towards a dustpan and brush.

'Two-Fingers says Sheila has an inner eye for this sort of thing.'

'What do you mean?'

'She's always lived here. Knows her way around. The living and the dead. He said. From a long line of white witches.'

'Sheila the cleaner?'

'We've all got to earn a crust.'

That night they cleared the bar of customers by a quarter to midnight. Simon, having decided to cash-up in the morning, locked the takings in the safe. Sheila, Bob-Job, and Two-Fingers set up the Ouija board around the corner from the area known as Annie's Well. Lauren stood over it, on the transparent Perspex cover, and looked down into the floodlit vertiginous tunnel. The hole beneath her feet carved out of the winking granite rock. She momentarily imagined smugglers, pirates, wreckers, and purveyors of contraband from hundreds of years ago. Annie leading them on, bellowing directions as they heaved barrel-loads of brandy and bales of fine silk along the tunnel dug through the cliff from cove to church town. Lauren was unsure of how she felt. Should she play along with this bringing-souls-back-from-the-dead charade? Or should she repeat her scepticism and make a statement by telling them she was going to bed? She felt something brush around her calves. She looked down and saw the black kitten looking up.

'Hello, Kitty. Have you come to help me make up my mind?'

The cat sat by her feet and looked up into her face.

Lauren shrugged. 'What?'

The cat mewed.

'Okay, okay if that's the way you want to play it? I'll stay. I'll stay for the séance. But no messing with me? Do you get it?'

Lauren moved towards the group, Simon had joined them, and the board was set up. Lauren turned back to look at the kitten. She had vanished.

'Simon said a bar glass was smashed,' said Two-Fingers.

'Yes, but I think it was too close to the edge and simply fell from the shelf,' said Lauren, not wanting to discuss the possibility that it might have been poltergeist activity. She couldn't bring herself to believe that. Nor did she want to feed imaginations that they may have a ghost in their midst.

'Do you know which sort?' Two-Fingers pushed.

'A brandy glass,' Simon said.

'Can you get another? The same. Exactly the same.'

'Why?' Lauren cut in, wondering what Two-Fingers was suggesting.

'We must use it as our marker. Annie has pointed out the vessel she wants us to use: a brandy glass.'

'Really? For goodness sake,' thought Lauren as she reluctantly moved to the bar, picked up a balloon snifter, brought it back to the table and gave it to Sheila. 'This is beyond hocus-pocus.'

'Let the board make the decision. Not you.' Sheila's words sounded mangled, like someone was gripping her windpipe. She continued, 'Sit and let us play.' She waved her hand, an imperious invite for Lauren to sit in the empty chair next to her.

Lauren sat down and took a breath. The air, she noted, was stale. If this was a warning sign, she did not heed it, preferring to accept that her imagination was making heavy weather of the sudden silence.

'Merciful spirits, we call out the name Annie George, landlady of the First and Last Inn, Sennen, Cornwall.' Now Sheila sounded oddly tremulous, even ethereal.

Lauren opened one eye and could see the seriousness of the group endeavour. Bob-Job's and Two-Fingers' hands were splayed – almost touching. Simon's eyes bolted shut. Sheila's head thrown back as if inviting in the devil himself.

Knocking.

She heard knocking.

Knock, knock, knock.

Knocking.

Where was it coming from? Was it real? Imagined?

Lauren's heart was thumping. She put her hand to her chest, trying to steady a wave of nerves.

What is this sorcery? You're all playing tricks with me? Yes, even you, Simon. Trying to scare me? No. No, I'm not having it.

Outside a barn owl shrieked. And something what – a bat? – banged against the old, mullioned window glass. Old glass that kept the old wives' tales outside.

Wives' tales? Odd. Why wives? Why not husbands? Never say rabbit in a boat. Never fish with a woman on board. I am not afraid. I am not afraid.

But, nevertheless, she shrieked. Like the barn owl. She shut her eyes, driving out her fear. Found confidence, opened them again.

All but Simon had gone. No Sheila, Bob-Job, no Two-Fingers. Vanished. Disappeared. Into the Ether. Like spirits in the night.

Simon leapt from his stool. It clattered behind him, breaking the silence.

He howled, 'We have to get out of here. Now. We have to go. Run, Lauren. I'm serious. Run for your life.'

Lauren found herself running. Running with Simon towards the door. She could see the car keys in his hand but had no idea of his plan. 'Simon?'

'We need to get out of here.'

Outside the rain lashed down, stinging her face. Cruel ice daggers, cutting and jabbing.

They made it to the car and fell inside.

Simon fumbled the start button. The car burst into life. He reversed out of a tight spot, whacking a metal bin. The sound metallic and scary. But nowhere near as scary as Lauren's scream.

'It's okay, Lauren, I've got this,' Simon yelled as he swung the car forward and roared across the tarmac towards the car park's exit. The rain battered the windscreen. The wipers grated. Lauren huddled and shivering.

Then...

'Stop the car!'

'What the...'

'I said stop the car.'

'Are you crazy?' Simon said, hackles raised, putting his foot down.

'Now, Simon. Now.'

Simon screeched the car to a halt and swung his face into hers. Hiatus.

'I have to go back for the kitten. She's Annie.'

'You are crazy.'

Lauren tugged at the door handle. The door flew open. Lauren bowled forward into the hedge. She heard Simon's car door slam but was already on her feet, running. She could taste blood in her mouth, where her front teeth had bitten into her bottom lip. Ferrous. Tannic. The wind blew bitter into her cheeks.

She must get back to the bar before Annie leaves. She knew this was her chance to help put things right. Whatever that meant.

Her legs flailed: ungainly strides against the cold coastal wind as it whipped across the top of the cliff. She must get back to the pub.

She could hear Simon yelling 'Lauren, come back,' but she paid no heed. She had to keep running. Running before she ran out of time. And she had to find the kitten. Find Annie. She'd look in the wardrobe first. The safe place. Annie's safe place for hundreds of years. For hundreds of years Annie has been waiting for her. She mustn't let Annie down. 'I'm coming,' Lauren cried into the bitter wind.

When Lauren opened the wardrobe door she found the kitten

crouched inside.

'Annie,' Lauren said. 'I know it's you.'

Lauren put her hand to the back of the wardrobe, feeling across the wooden panels, searching for a trap or a clue. Nothing. The kitten mewed. Lauren look down and picked her up and smiled. 'I get it. Your spirit is still here, isn't it? This is where you tried to hide.' The kitten wriggled out of Lauren's arms and ran out of the bedroom. Lauren followed and found herself back at the Ouija board.

The pub door flew open. Simon stood in the frame. The sound of the wind sudden and whistling. But, when he spoke, the wind dropped, and his voice was calm and warm, 'Crazy or not. I can't leave you here.'

Lauren was about to reply she was glad that he had come back when the kitten clambered onto Sheila's chair and seemed to set the brandy snifter racing across the Ouija board. Lauren and Simon watched as it spelt out the truth.

A shaft of morning sunshine picked out the engraving on the ancient slate gravestone.

Sheila Trembath.

Wise Woman of West Penwith

Buried here in the year of our Lord 1888.

'I wonder how she died?'

'It doesn't say.'

'No. But weird that she's right next to Robert Hosken and Samuel Hicks.'

'Bob-Job and Two-Fingers?'

'Yeah, like they all hang around in a pack, even in death.'

'I'll miss them.'

'No you won't. Bar bores, remember?'

'Who'll do the cleaning now?'

'We'll get someone. Okay, so where's Annie? In the car park, under the outhouse?' asked Simon.

'Here. Right here.'

'I thought she was buried in unconsecrated ground outside of the church.'

Lauren looked down at the small patch of ground between Bob-Job's and Sheila's graves. 'That's what makes me believe that Annie's version of the story is the truth. They buried her here in the churchyard to make amends. Yes, she did report Dionysius Williams and he was tried, but being a toff, he got off lightly with a knuckle rapped and a few nights in gaol. But she was in danger of losing her home and livelihood, and for my money, he was fair game. The rest of it was his revenge. Right down to her brother-in-law. How perfect to get rid of both of them in one hit. Annie was buried inside the grounds of the church in an unmarked grave. But not any longer.'

Lauren placed the wooden stake she was carrying at the head of the patch of ground and drove it through the grass and into the hard earth. She attached a second piece of wood until it was perpendicular and resembled a cross. On it, a small sign.

Annie George

R.I.P.

'We going to give it a go then?' asked Simon.

'Why not? I think we have Annie's approval,' said Lauren.

'What about the rest of the ghosts?'

'I think they'll be a long time dead – from now on.'

'The kitten?'

'Will be a cat in no time. Come on then, let's go serve beer.'

Simon slipped his hand into Lauren's as the couple headed back to the First and Last Inn next door. Lauren looked across to Simon, smiled, and thought rather coyly about the potential of a very different thing going bump in the night.

The Ghost of Dozmary Pool

Roz Watkins

Dad's been a mess since Mum died, so I was hardly even surprised when he announced he was moving us to Cornwall to live in a falling-down cottage in a bog. I mean, that's not how he put it, but I got the subtext. I'm good like that – officially, according to my English teacher.

Mum had been ill for a long time. I think I cried myself to sleep every night for a year, so when she actually died, it was almost as if I had no more tears left. Whereas Dad held it together, for me I guess, and now he can't manage that anymore. Even though I'm only ten, I feel like I'm looking after him.

It's the start of the summer holidays and I'm due to go to a new school next term anyway, so Dad says it won't be that disruptive moving me to a different county. But I heard a teacher saying it would be disruptive because I don't make friends easily. I think the teacher was right because I was really sad leaving my best friend, Maia, who I've known since I was five.

When we pull up outside our new house, it's as bad as I thought. Dad said it's from the seventeenth century, which means a year starting with a sixteen, so totally old. And it looks it. It's made of dark lumps of stone and the roof's a slimy green and it has tiny little rotting wooden windows. It's half of a big house split in two. Our house and the one attached to it are the only things I can see for miles around. We're in a place called Bodmin Moor, which is famous for being remote and having a beast.

'Here we are, Sophie!' Dad says, in a fake-happy voice. 'Let's go in and get a cup of tea.'

When I open the car door, a gust of wind slams it shut again, even though it's supposed to be summer. I push the door open again. It already feels like this place has it in for me.

'Luckily, I had the foresight to put the kettle and some teabags in the car,' Dad says.

'Can I have some Coke?' I say. It's just a routine we have. I ask and he says no.

'No,' Dad says.

'Is there a shop or a town?' One of the only times I'd get Coke at my old place was if I walked the long way to the shop along the footpath.

'Not close to here,' Dad says. 'But there are lots of beautiful walks. A lake and some woods. And I brought biscuits!' He turns and rummages on the back seat, then whips out a pack of fig rolls, as if that makes up for me having no friends, a crappy house, no shops, and also no mum.

He maintains the fake cheeriness just long enough to get us and the kettle and the fig rolls into the house and then disappears to go and be depressed somewhere, so I head to the kitchen to make us both a cup of tea.

The kitchen's weird and old. There's a big stone fireplace, flagstones on the floor, and a black metal thing that I think is the oven. The electricity works, but Dad didn't show that much foresight after all, because there's no milk. I make black tea.

I take the tea through into the front room where Dad is. The room's really grim with a worn green carpet on the floor that looks like creatures live in it, and a horrible dark painting over the fireplace that's so dirty I can't even work out what it's supposed to be. Our furniture's arriving later with the removal men so Dad's on the windowsill, which is huge. He's sitting sideways and staring at all the nothingness outside. I hand him his tea and he says, 'Thanks, Sophe. You're a good girl.' But he doesn't even look at me.

The removal men take most of the afternoon unloading all our stuff into the cottage. I make them cups of black tea and coffee, and they eat all the fig rolls.

By the time they're done, it's pretty late and I just want to go to bed. Even though it's July, there's mist drifting around the cottage and a noise outside that sounds like someone screaming. Dad says it's an owl or a fox, but it sounds human to me.

It's so cold I fill a hot water bottle that I amazingly found in a box and take it to bed. I want my fluffy cat, Munchkin, who

I still like even though I'm too old for soft toys, but she's in a different box somewhere and I can't find her. I can't even find my nightshirt or toothbrush. I get into bed in my clothes and listen to the screaming outside and cry for the first time in weeks.

I wake up suddenly, eyes wide open. It's pitch dark, and feels like it's the middle of the night, even though I don't know what time it is because I haven't unpacked my Alexa. The hairs on the back of my neck are standing on end and it's really cold. Like, way colder than it should be in July. My heart's beating really fast.

The duvet's half off me, but when I try to pull it into place, I can't move. My arms feel like they're glued to the bed. Now I'm really scared and my heart's beating so hard I think I might die. My head's turned to one side, towards my door, and then I see something so terrifying, I want to scream but I can't scream or move or anything. I'm stuck to the bed staring at this... thing.

It's in the doorway, looking at me. It's a man, but his skin is grey and seems to be peeling off his face, and his eyes are black and dead-looking. There's a smell like rotting seaweed.

I wrench my head around and make my arms and legs work and I scream and scream.

Dad's at my bedside, saying, 'It was just a dream, Sophe, just a dream. You're fine. I'm here now.'

And I'm sobbing and saying, 'It wasn't a dream. He was here. A man. He was in the doorway.'

And, in the end, we agree to disagree, but Dad drags his mattress through and sleeps on the floor of my room with me.

In the morning, the thing with the man seems a lot less real. Dad says there's something called Sleep Paralysis where you're half awake and half asleep. You think you're awake but your body's still paralysed like when you're dreaming, and you see scary stuff like in a dream. And it happens when you've been upset and not sleeping well, which is me at the moment. So, I decide it must have been that.

Dad forces me to go for a really long walk on the moors. Most of the time, it feels like we're walking on tussocks of grass coming out of a basic swamp, so it's not a great walk. On the way back, we go past this place called Dozmary Pool, which is close to our house. It's surrounded by brown hills and there's mist over the water. When I look at it, I get a nervous tingle in my stomach. The pool is really black. Dad says it's just the reflection of the sky, but the water's a lot blacker than the sky. There's a weird smell like something that's gone off in the back of the fridge. Dad says the pool's something to do with King Arthur and tells me a long and pretty boring story, which I've forgotten.

When we get home, we do a load of unpacking which is hard work and really sad because Mum's not here. Neither me or Dad want to do it, but we do the basics so we can watch the TV and cook some pasta and, at least when I go to bed, I have my nightshirt and toothbrush and also Munchkin the cat.

I'm scared to go to sleep at first. Dad says it'll be fine, and he takes his mattress back to his room. He says it was only a dream and it won't happen again and he kisses me on the forehead and I feel like he does care but, even so, I'm dismissed. He has his own stuff to deal with.

I wake again in the night. I'm not paralysed this time. I look at my clock and it's 3.03 a.m. I'm scared to turn my head the other way to look at the doorway. But then I smell it again. Like washing that's been left out in the rain, or a mouldy corner of an old house.

I turn my head really, really slowly. My hand flies up to my face to stop my scream. He's there, and he's closer. He's taken a step into my room. He's soaking wet and he has seaweed draped over him. I stop myself screaming, but I let out a kind of whimper. I'm so scared I think I'll pass out, but still I don't scream.

And then he's gone.

The next day, I tell Dad I don't want to live in this house anymore. I want to go back home and stay with Maia, or with Grandma, or basically anywhere except here. I tell him the man came again and he says it was a dream and then I'm shouting at him saying it wasn't a dream, it was real. And he's not listening so I bolt out into the small garden behind the house and run to the far end and throw myself into the mud and just scream with frustration.

A small voice. 'Are you okay?'

I jump up in a panic that someone saw me like this, and there's a girl about my age in the next-door garden, looking over the stone wall. I quickly wipe my face and say, 'I'm fine.'

I'd sort of forgotten that there was a whole other house attached to ours.

'What's your name?' the girl says.

'Sophie.'

'I'm Tess. Do you want to come into my garden?'

I'm about to say *No*, out of habit, but I don't want to go back inside with Dad, who doesn't care about me, and there's nowhere else to go since I have no friends here and there are no shops or anything apart from a disgusting black pool. So I shrug and say, 'All right.'

Tess gestures to a low area of the wall between our gardens

and I clamber over.

She's got long tangled red hair and looks a bit of a mess, which makes me feel better because I've basically just been lying in mud, crying and screaming. She has a sketch pad and shows me an ink drawing of a beetle that she's done. It's so realistic it makes me shudder. I can see the little hairs on its legs and its huge eyes.

She puts her drawing down and says, 'Does he come to you in the night as well?'

I freeze.

'I heard you screaming,' she says.

I don't like to look people in the eye, but I end up doing it for just a moment. Her eyes are green. 'The *man*?' I say.

She nods.

Then I hear Dad shouting for me and he sounds like he's in a panic, so I say, 'Bye,' and jump back over the wall.

Over the next couple of weeks, Dad only seems to get worse. He's supposed to be working from home, but he just sits and stares out of the window most of the time. He manages to order online food deliveries and between us we cook enough food to survive, but that's basically all. He's made no attempt to make the house any nicer or even clean it. One evening I go into his room and he's sitting on the bed counting out paracetamols and there's a bottle of whisky on the bedside table. When he sees me, he stops and shoves everything in a drawer, but I know it's not good. He's in such a bad way that I don't tell him about the man again, even though he comes every night and each time he's a little closer to my bed, dripping water on the floor and smelling wet and rotten and staring at me.

Dad pays so little attention to me that I end up spending most of my time with Tess. She says the man comes to her too. She says he's the ghost of a man who used to live in our house hundreds of years ago, before it was split in two. She even has a name for him. Jan Tregeagle.

Dad has at least got the WiFi going which is just as well because there's no mobile signal. So one day I manage to borrow his phone and sneak off to my bedroom to google Jan Tregeagle. He seems to have been a real man in the seventeenth century, but everyone hated him and some say he murdered his wife, Emily ('née Swann' which I found out means her name before she got married) and her daughter, when he found out the daughter wasn't his. Apparently, he sold his soul to the devil and now he has to sit by the pool forever, trying to empty it with a leaky shell. According to one website, 'his howls of anguish can be heard reverberating around the valley.'

I sit back on my bed, thinking about the screaming I hear on the moor. But it must be foxes or owls, like Dad said. I take the phone back to Dad and tell him about the man who used to live here, but I don't say he's been coming to me in the night.

The next time I see Tess, she says, 'We've got to get rid of him. I found a spell we can do to send him on his way.'

Part of me still doesn't really even believe in the man, but the other part of me knows he's getting closer to my bed each night. How can I be so scared of something I don't even believe in?

'We have to go down to the pool at midnight and do the spell,' Tess says.

Eventually I agree to go with Tess and do her spell. I sneak out just before midnight and we head for the pool. The moon's bright, so it's not too hard to follow the path through the boggy field, and

I don't need my torch. The water's blacker than ever, with just a faint silver reflection glistening on it. I feel like cold fingers are touching my back.

We chant the spell that Tess taught me. As we say the words, the water in the pool starts moving. I force myself not to run away. There's a great churning in the pool and then he's there. The man I see each night. He's partly in the water, but his head and upper body are poking out. There's a terrible, angry expression on his face and then he lets out this ear-shattering scream and it turns into words and he's screaming, 'No! I can't leave here! I'll go to Hell!'

We keep chanting and he keeps screaming and I've never been so scared, but Tess is being brave, so I don't move even though I want to run and run and never come back to this awful place.

Finally, Tess stops chanting, and the man sinks back into the water.

I look round at Tess and she's letting out huge gulping sobs that go right into her chest. I try to put my arm round her even though I hate that, but she moves away. I tell her it'll be okay, even though I don't think it will be okay.

I'm back home and in bed by 2 a.m. An hour or so later, I'm awake again and he's there. He's really close to my bed now, dripping water and smelling of dark things that live underwater. And I realise he's whispering something. It sounds like, 'In the secret place.'

I'm so exhausted, I just close my eyes and wait for him to go.

But the next morning, I tell Tess what he said, and she thinks she knows what he meant.

'Is there a painting over the fireplace in your front room?' she says.

I nod. Dad hasn't even bothered to move the horrible painting. 'See if there's a cubby hole behind it.'

I try to get Tess to help me, but she refuses to come into my house. I can hardly blame her, with the state of my dad. I go inside and drag a chair through from the kitchen and shove it underneath the horrible painting and climb up. In the daylight, I can see it's a painting of the pool. And with a jolt, I realise there's a faint figure rising up out of the water, just like we saw last night. I lift the painting, which is a lot heavier than it looks, and drop it on the floor. Tess was right. There's a tiny door behind it. At first it doesn't want to shift, but I manage to work the catch loose and open it. There's something inside that looks like parchment. Holding my breath and praying Dad won't emerge from his 'office' (not that he seems to do any work) I take it out and run into the garden to find Tess. I don't bother to try and put the horrible painting back. That needs burning.

We look at the parchment together. The writing looks ancient but it's readable. *Spell for ghosts in limbo to remove said unfortunate individual from this corporeal world so it is as if they had never been born, and they avoid eternal damnation and torment in the fires of Hell. Spell must be spoken with profound conviction by a living person.*

Tess sees it and lets out a kind of sigh. 'Oh! It's because he'll go to hell for what he did. His only choices are hell or this purgatory he's in now, because of the awful things he did.'

'So he wants us to do a spell to make it like he never even existed?' As I say it, it seems crazy, but I'm ready to try anything to get rid of the man.

'Maybe that's why he keeps coming to you in the night,' Tess says.

It's cloudy and much darker than last night. I keep stumbling into swampy areas because Tess doesn't have a torch and I shine mine at her feet to be nice, and then I can't see where I'm going. By the time we get to the pool I'm freezing.

I pull out the parchment and direct my torch at it.

'You read it,' Tess says.

'We'll read it together.'

But when we start reading, her voice is super quiet so it's only mine that projects out over the pool.

And then I see words that I didn't notice before. I could swear they weren't there earlier. *You must enter the pool.*

I look at the black surface of the water and think of that *thing* inside it. But then it's as if something takes over my body, and I move forwards. Tess comes with me, and we slowly edge our way in. It's beyond the cold that makes you scream. It's so cold the shock of it nearly paralyses me, but I keep walking. Tess is brave – she doesn't even flinch.

I hold the parchment above me and, once we're up to our chests, I start chanting the spell. My voice trembles, but gets steadier as I go. I seem to be in a kind of trance. I just keep chanting.

It feels as if the water's bubbling underneath me and around me, as if I'm in a cauldron, but a freezing cold one. My legs are weak and numb, and it feels like there's a cold hand squeezing my insides, but I keep chanting. The whole pool is bubbling and spitting. An owl lets out a shriek and flies away.

There's a shout and then a huge spurt of water as if there's a volcano or something in the pool. Jan Tregeagle shoots up out of the water and looks at me with those dead eyes. I can't force myself to look away. We stare at each other and I feel like I might pass out from terror. But then his body goes pale and turns to mist which sinks back into the pool. The churning of the water stops and there are just a few bubbles.

'Oh my God,' Tess whispers. 'He's really gone.'

I take a huge gasp of air and it's as if my trance has gone and I'm so cold I think I'll die. I lunge towards the edge of the pool and drag myself out.

I see light in the distance and realise dawn is on the way. We must have been here hours. Everything that's happened is so strange and scary, my brain doesn't properly believe it.

Tess and I glance at each other and then stagger home.

When we get back to our house, I see a woman through Tess's front window, waving excitedly at us. The light in the kitchen is a warm yellow and I see a couple of candles flickering behind her. I realise it's the first time I've seen Tess's mum, and I feel a sharp stab of jealousy at how happy she seems, compared to my dad. She doesn't seem angry that we've been out all night and that we're drenched with stinking pond water.

Tess looks as if a huge weight has been lifted from her. 'He won't come in the night any more!' she says, and practically dances towards her front door, dripping on the flagstone path.

Just as she's about to go in, she stops, turns to me and stares really hard at me. 'Thank you, Sophie,' she says. 'You've saved my life.'

'All right,' I say. 'Let's see if it worked first.'

She gives me a huge beaming smile and disappears into her house.

Once she's gone, I immediately feel less cheerful, and start panicking that Dad'll have a fit at me for going out in the middle of the night. I open the door tentatively, but there's no sign of him.

I'm really tired so I go to bed for a couple of hours.

When I get up, it's almost ten. Nobody came to me while I was asleep. I realise I really believe the man's gone, and that I'll be okay now. I feel lighter than I have for ages. I head for the kitchen and find Dad standing in front of the weird iron stove thing, stirring porridge in a pan.

He turns round to look at me and his face is different. More like it used to be, before everything with Mum. He says, 'I'm really sorry, Sophie. I've been a terrible dad to you these last few weeks.'

'No, you haven't,' I say, even though he actually has.

He puts the wooden spoon down and gives me a serious look. 'I know you saw me with those pills and that's just…' He claws a hand through his hair. 'Unforgiveable. It's unforgiveable.'

I shrug. 'It's okay.'

'I'm better now,' he says. 'On the mend. You don't have to worry about me any more.'

I feel quite awkward. I give a little nod and smile. It's weird how Dad seems happier too, now Jan Tregeagle has gone. For the first time since Mum died, I think we might cope, just me and Dad.

'They've put a *For Sale* sign against next door,' he says. 'Hopefully we'll get nice neighbours.'

'What?' I rush to the kitchen window and look out. He's right. There's a sign planted firmly against the front gatepost. 'Are the people leaving?' I say.

Dad frowns. 'What people?'

'The woman. The girl. Tess!'

'That house has been derelict for years, Sophe. Nobody lives there.'

I charge out of the kitchen door and into next-door's front garden. I peer through the kitchen window, remembering the smiling woman, the warm glow of the candles. All I see is dust and cobwebs and walls covered in black mould.

My heart pounds. I run back to my house and yell at Dad, 'What about my friend?'

I'm crying, and I tell Dad about Tess and how the man who came in the night was the ghost of Jan Tregeagle.

Dad hugs me and tells me it's all okay. But then he says, 'Who's Jan Tregeagle?'

'We talked about him! He used to live in this house. He killed his wife and stepdaughter! You know who he is.'

'Look, Sophe, sit down. Let me make you a drink.'

I sit down but demand that Dad gives me his phone. He's so shocked at my attitude that he hands it over.

I quickly google Jan Tregeagle. But I can't find anything. It's as if he never existed. I search and search and can't find any sign of him. I remember the smell of him, seaweed and damp. I picture him turning to mist and sinking into the depths of the black pool, just a few bubbles rising as he went down.

I look up at Dad and frown. 'He's not here.'

'Was it another bad dream?' Dad says.

I hand the phone back.

Did I imagine it all?

Or did we do it? Did Tess and I really make it as if Jan Tregeagle never existed?

But who is Tess? How can her house be derelict and unlived-in? And I clearly saw her mother through the kitchen window, glowing in the candlelight.

And it slowly comes to me. I didn't think I believed in ghosts, but I saw Jan Tregeagle's. And if now he never existed, he can't have killed his wife and stepdaughter after all. I dredge into the depths of my brain for Jan Tregeagle's wife's name before she married him. I know I read it on one of the webpages which don't exist anymore. It comes to me. Swann! Emily Swann.

I google *Tess Swann*. And there she is. Daughter of Emily. One of the most notable female artists of the seventeenth century, famous for her hyper-realistic drawings of insects.

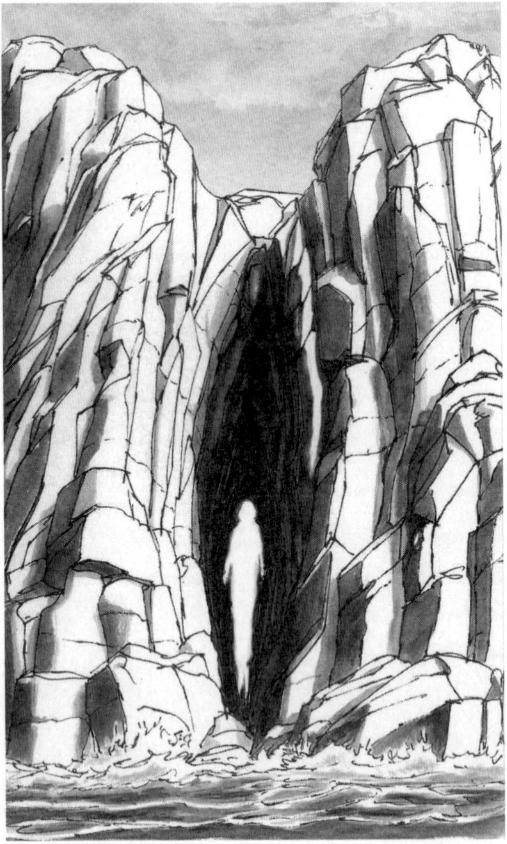

The Black Zawn

Jane Johnson

The view out of the window was nothing like the one Gina had pictured when she'd booked herself and Josh into the Airbnb for a few days' climbing on the Cornish coast. She'd expected at least a sea glimpse, but all they had seen was a succession of grey-slate roofs and, while the sight and sound of seagulls and jackdaws on the chimney pots signalled that they were a long way from North London, it was not quite the romantic setting she'd hoped might reset their faltering relationship. Still, the seafront was only a short walk away, and the tiny fisherman's cottage, though sparsely furnished, was clean and bright.

The front door banged open, and Josh huffed into view, a rucksack slung over one shoulder, a bulging holdall in each hand. 'I had to park miles away!' he complained. 'There was no space in the harbour carpark, and the big one charges a tenner a day: they must hate tourists down here!'

'You could have left the climbing gear in the car,' Gina said gently, but her partner of three years glared at her.

'Are you kidding? It's worth more than your bloody car!'

Funny how the Renault always became 'her' car whenever there was a problem. Josh had given up his car when he moved in with her. 'No point in paying two lots of insurance and road tax, let alone two parking permits!' But much like her flat, it had now seemed to pass into his purview. She hardly even got to drive it any more, and whenever she did, Josh would wince and hiss if she got too close to the kerb or another vehicle, his knee would bob as he stepped on the imaginary brake. To avoid arguments, she just let him drive. In the same way, she had stopped voicing most of her opinions, never wore jeans that were too tight or tops that were too short or heels that were too high. But she told herself all these small concessions were worth it: Josh was handsome and fit, a fearless climber, a successful broker and, most of the time, they got along well enough. If occasionally he got a bit rough during sex, she would remember how when she'd told Tasha about one incident that had left thumb marks on her neck, she'd replied, 'Lucky you. I wouldn't mind Josh going a bit Christian Grey on me!'

She and Tasha weren't really friends any more, and indeed most of her other friends seemed to have drifted away, got married, had babies, moved out of London. It was lucky that she loved climbing: it was how she had met Josh – at the Castle climbing gym in Green Lanes. She'd been leading a 5c route up some pretty small holds, with Hannah holding her rope, when this tall, blond man had started calling up encouragement – 'Reach for the little incut and transfer your weight onto your right foot!' She'd tried to do what he suggested, but she needed to be ten centimetres taller to follow his instructions and had gone flying, almost pulling the belaying Han off her feet, and had swung from the rope laughing with the shock of the fall. After that, she'd seen Josh every time she visited the gym, and they had fallen into one another's company and then into Gina's bed.

That evening as they ate fish and chips at the village pub, Josh pored over the guidebook, his fingers tracing route descriptions as he scrutinised the best venue for the following day. 'Black Zawn,' he declared at last. 'You ab down to the wavecut platform. There are some awesome climbs, and we can ease in with an easy one to start with.' He pushed the guidebook across the table to her.

The topographical photo showed a dramatic looking cliff looming forty metres or so out of the sea. The routes were white-dotted to either side of a black void, which appeared to be a huge cave. Black Zawn. It didn't sound very appealing, and the only way in being an abseil down to sea level meant the only way out was to climb up. What if it was too hard for her? And she hated caves: something about the chill, dank air inside them made her imagine monsters lurking out of sight. Just the thought of it made Gina shiver. She would be left alone on the wavecut platform right by the cave while Josh was climbing.

'Lovely,' she said, though her guts roiled.

The following morning, after a difficult night in which it turned out the mattress was too soft for Josh's back and he had ended up sleeping on the floor, dawned bright and sunny. Over breakfast, Gina scanned one of the local interest pamphlets left for visitors in the cottage: *Ancient Sites and Tales of West Penwith*. Goodness, there were a lot of stone circles and burial chambers in this part of Cornwall, she thought as she read through it. Iron Age settlements, sacred wells, menhirs that purported to be witches or pipers who had been turned to stone, maidens petrified in an endless dance, devils trapped down deep shafts, sorcerers hanged and beheaded, vast white hares that galloped across the clifftops or down deeply wooded valleys, presaging doom. It seemed that Cornwall saved all its weirdness for its Wild West. She stowed the pamphlet into her climbing sack: something to read over her packed lunch.

The view from the top of the crag was astonishing: the sea stretching to a distant horizon, shallows and currents painted in shades of teal, turquoise, and aquamarine. Had Gina been here just to take in the sights, to walk the coast path with a picnic and a beach visit to look forward to, she would have felt ecstatic, with the breeze whipping her hair into her face, seabirds planing sideways on an upcurrent, and the scent of coconut boiling off the gorse flowers. But one look down into the deep zawn was enough to quench her joy. Although the rockface was in the sun, the bottom section was split in two by the black slash of the cave, a yawning maw that seemed to suck in all the light around it.

Rather than concentrate on her fear, she focused on setting up a safe abseil point, irritated as always by Josh's insistence on retying her knots and yanking on the camming devices. He really didn't trust her to do anything. Though some of that was her own fault: it was simply easier to let him take the lead and show off his expertise.

That first step backwards into the air was always the worst thing, trusting your weight to a rope and abseil device, but within a few metres, Gina was enjoying the controlled freefall, letting the rope pay out smoothly till her feet were safely planted on the platform of rock at the foot of the climbs, a substantial shelf of rose-gold granite studded with quartz and mica that glinted in the sun. Here, they spread out their kit and uncoiled the ropes. Josh walked along beneath the cliff, shading his eyes to scope out the routes, guidebook in hand. He would spend ages doing this – assessing the moves and the difficulties, the resting points and belays, dipping his hands in his chalk-bag and trying out a sequence or two, till he had an entire route programmed in his head. It gave Gina a little time to take in her surroundings and enjoy the proximity of the sparkling waves, to examine the colonies of barnacles and limpets, to eat some of her sandwich and scan a bit more of the pamphlet.

'On the Pendhu Headland,' she read, 'are the remains of a prehistoric funerary cairn or chambered tomb which appears to have been used and reused for various unknown purposes through Neolithic times, the Bronze Age and well into the Iron Age. Fragments of Beaker culture pottery have been recovered in the vicinity. It is thought that the Beaker folk migrated to Cornwall from the Eurasian Steppe, bringing with them genes for paler eyes and skin than the resident inhabitants, with their olive skin and dark hair and eyes; and techniques for refining metals, and smelting copper. A copper dagger and jewellery from the era can be seen in the Royal Cornwall Museum. These were excavated from the cave in the Black Zawn, amongst many objects indicating that the site had been an area reserved for the sacred burial of individuals of high status, including the legendary White Lady, who was interred wearing long necklaces of ivory and copper beads, though the dating of the bones remains imprecise, complicated by the possibility of there being several different corpses interred in the cave.'

Gina closed the booklet, wishing now she had not read this entry at all. She did not want to climb on some prehistoric burial site. Bad things always happened in stories when people trespassed on sacred ground. She looked back towards the cave and was horrified to see Josh swinging monkey-like from its roof, six or seven metres off the ground, biceps bulging and climbing shoes finding purchase as he moved horizontally from one side of the shadowed opening to the other. He climbed down the stepped wall, jumped the last few feet back to the platform, shook out his forearms and loped back towards her, grinning.

'Wow, this place is quite something!' He held out his hands towards her and she could see rock-rash and traces of blood seeping through the chalk which he had used to improve his grip. 'Loads of amazing crystals in this granite, but they don't half cut you up!'

Like this, with his golden hair glowing in the sunlight, his blue eyes lit with enthusiasm, and his tanned, muscular arms on show, he looked, Gina thought, like a young god. Even under the artificial lights at the Castle, he had seemed so to her, three years ago, as tall and beautifully proportioned as a Greek statue, though rather better endowed. Something like love flooded through her, and for a moment she felt happy to be here with him, about to embark on another adventure up the rock, on the safe end of the rope.

Josh selected the gear he would need for the route, garlanding his brightly coloured harness with cams, nuts, and wires, bandoliered with slings and carabiners, and together they carried the ropes to the foot of the climb he had selected: Lord of the Waves, E1 5b. They tied on, Gina ran the rope through her belay device, and Josh set off, moving as elegantly in the vertical plane as he did on the ground. It was like an upward dance, Gina thought, watching him placing gear and clipping into it, moving fluently. Soon, he was at the top, making a belay and taking in the rope, ready for Gina to follow. As soon as she was on the route, she could feel how steep and strenuous it was going to be; within metres her forearms were aching, and when she had to stop to wrestle one of the pieces of protection he had placed rather too well, she was soon pumped and sweating.

'Hurry up!' Josh yelled, unsympathetic.

Sighing, Gina finally managed to poke the wire from the crack, shook out her arm, and carried on. At the hardest part of the climb, she had to balance precariously around the side of the arete rather than take it head on and was berated by her partner for 'cheating'. He hauled so hard on the rope that her harness cut into her groin, making her shout with pain. Looking down, she could see they were traversing directly above the cave and her stomach lurched.

'Christ, Gina, come up! Just swing off the flake. Don't be such a girl.'

Gina stared up at him, then away. She couldn't let him see her cry. She brushed tears away, then rubbed her hand on the rock to dry it. As she did so, she felt a slow wave of anger roll through her. An unfamiliar emotion, it seemed to originate from somewhere so deep inside her that she barely recognised it as her own. It powered her up the remaining section of rock and back down again on the abseil to the wavecut platform. It even gave her the confidence to suggest that she might lead the next route, pointing out to Josh a shield of rock to the right of the cave, which lay at a gentler angle.

Josh scoffed. 'That's a girl's route. I didn't come here to get led up a fucking VS.'

Instead, he pointed out a climb called Excaliburner, graded at E3: a hard, steep route that Gina knew she would have difficulty seconding. Josh knew she didn't enjoy being pushed to her limits – and beyond – on sea cliff climbs. Sometimes she wondered if he did it on purpose, imposing his superior strength on her – another form of torment, of domination. She wondered when she had got so feeble that she couldn't seem to exert her own will. After all, when she'd met Josh she'd been outgoing – even exuberant – social, funny, confident. She was doing well at life, was financially independent, had a loving family, a load of lively friends, and could lead a mean HVS, even – if the angle and delicacy were right – a decent E1. Somehow all these things had been pared away from her. No more drinks with the girls or weekends with her parents; no more dinner parties or evenings at the pub. No more dancing the night away or trips to conferences abroad. She tried not to think too much about the difference in her life now to what it had been before Josh. When she did think about it, sometimes she wanted to cry. Then she would give herself a stern talking to and remind herself that Josh was handsome and successful and that other girls watched him with cats' eyes when they were out together.

But about a fortnight before their holiday, he had hurt her...

She pulled her mind away from the memory of that night and focused on the laces of her climbing shoes: she'd need them really tight for this route, no matter the pain.

They made their way to the base of Excaliburner, on the steeper face to the right of the big cave. Standing beneath it, her neck craning to take in the details of the route, Gina felt a stab of dread. It was too hard for her: she'd never be able to get up it. Her arms were already pumped from the previous climb, her muscles hard with lactic acid. She would slip and fall, at the mercy of the rope, with Josh having to haul her like a lump of meat. She could taste the humiliation already.

But there was no time to dwell: Josh was placing his first piece of gear, and dutifully she paid the rope through the belay device and watched him move past the crack onto the open face. Ten metres later, he was protecting the first crux: a bulge of dark granite that led to an overhanging shield of rock. More rope, Josh jerking it roughly, shouting something indistinct.

He made short work of the bulge and started on the overhang, moving with his usual fluidity and precision. Gina was sure she wouldn't be able to second that steep section; she just knew it, with a dread that sat like a stone inside her, weighing her down.

A few minutes later Josh was at the top, pulling in the rope till it was snug on Gina's harness. Three tugs signalled that it was her turn to climb. 'Climbing!' she called, following the protocol, but the air swallowed the sound, carried it away into the black recesses of the cave.

By the time she reached the bulging shoulder of granite, Gina's arms were on fire – as the name of the route had suggested might be the case – and her hand shook as she tried to release the piece of gear Josh had placed there. Removing it took the last of her strength. She bent her head in against the rock and shuddered. The rock accepted her despair, but gave it back as defiance. Gina shook her arms out, right then left, rolled her shoulders, assessed the holds, and tackled the bulge, one toe in a crack, the other bridged out to balance her. She made a step up and jammed a hand into a tight crack, pulled, and swung herself up. For a moment, both feet lost touch with the granite, then she brought her knees up and somehow – somehow – she was standing straight and clambering over the bulge. Exhilaration flooded through her. She had done it! It was just the first crux, but it appeared to be the most brutal part of the route, and she was over it!

Buoyed by her unexpected success, Gina unwedged her hand, retrieved the camming device Josh had placed, clipped it onto her gear loops and started to move up the shield.

'Get a bloody move on!' yelled Josh from the top of the route.

He pulled at the ropes, nearly jerking Gina off her precarious stance.

'Hey, Josh, don't! Give me a bit of slack!'

The rope looped down: he had deliberately let out too much now; another sort of punishment. If she fell here, she would drop back down past the bulge, banging herself on the way. So: she couldn't fall, she thought angrily. She wouldn't give him that satisfaction.

Gritting her teeth, Gina reached for a small hold. It was only when her fingers slipped on its edge that she realised she was bleeding. The crack in which she had inserted her hand to pull herself up over the crux must have been studded with crystals, cutting into her knuckles. She did her best to lick the blood away, tasting the tang of the rich, briny substance on her tongue, but more welled up and bright drops fell onto the granite, onto the patches of golden lichen that rosetted its surface, staining it crimson. More dripped into the deep crack below. She had the sense of her blood falling *through* the rock, somehow, and then on, into the void. Into the great maw of the cave below, down through its dark and ancient air, unseen, unheard, unknown, till at last it hit the cavern floor a hundred feet below.

As it struck, Gina felt a charge run through her, a jolt of energy. Her pain and burgeoning anger, all the unspoken suffering accrued over the past years was suddenly suffused by vivid memories of what Josh had done to her a fortnight ago. She had been tired, worn out by a hard week at work, but he wouldn't take no for an answer and, in the end, she had just lain back to let him do it so she could sleep. Perhaps it was her passivity that had infuriated him. Whatever it was, she saw his eyes turn a dull, shark-black before he flipped her over on her front and, with one hand holding her face down into the pillow so she could hardly breathe, rammed the fingers of his other hand up into her till she felt something split. Even as he pushed inside her, she knew that he was deliberately trying to hurt her, that there was a kind of rage-filled hatred driving him. Afterwards, crying in the bathroom, she had asked herself what she had done to make him hate and despise her so. She could find no answer, and the next day Josh had been completely normal, a bit grumpy, but nothing out of the ordinary, had made her breakfast, even sprinkled chocolate on the froth of her coffee, and she had done her best to close the experience away in a box and not think about it again.

But now, her anger and pain seemed to merge with something ancient, something dormant in the heart of Black Zawn. The next time Josh swore at her, she swore back, resolute and defiant. 'Josh! Take the bloody rope in!'

She could feel his anger as if it zinged down the rope like a charge of electricity. And then the rope looped once more as, instead of taking it in till it was tight on her harness and she could climb in safety, Josh let out yet more, a great loop that billowed on the breeze. And then, with horror, she watched as he let go of his belay device, unzipped his jeans and, aiming right at her, pissed down the route. She watched the arc of golden urine sparkle in the sunlight and strike the rock in hot dribbles that flecked the granite in front of her, ran down between patches of lichen.

For a moment, Gina stood in her now life-threatening position on the rock, stunned by disbelief. Then, self-preservation kicked in and she took the camming device from her gear loop, rammed it into a crack and clipped into it. Now, anchored to the rock with at least a degree of safety, she tilted her head back and yelled, 'You evil fucking monster!'

The roar she emitted sounded nothing like her own voice: it held a deep resonance, and the words did not even sound like English.

Up above, Josh was doing something with his hands. She couldn't quite see what until she leaned out from the rock. He was untying! Untying from the belay. Dropping the rope, which snaked out into the air and whizzed past her, accelerating as it went. What the hell? Was he just going to leave her here, marooned on the rockface, thirty-five metres up a granite sea-cliff?

Then Josh turned back and gazed down at her, his expression completely blank and, as if driven by some unseen force, stepped off the clifftop, into thin air. He plummeted right past Gina, feet first, without a sound, without even waving his arms or trying to grab the rock, or doing anything at all to save himself. Down, and down, dropping like a stone, or a statue, till he hit the wavecut platform far below with a dull, unsurvivable thud.

Gina looked down. Part of her still believed Josh was up above, larking around on the clifftop, pissing down the route 'for a laugh'. But another part of her knew that she was staring at his broken corpse. A dark pool of liquid leaked from his head, dyeing the golden corona of hair, ran in runnels off the edge of the platform into the lapping sea, which sucked it up, retreated, then returned for more.

And then, seemingly out of nowhere, a wave rose up out of the serene surface, crashed over the platform and carried Josh away into the zawn, trailing blossoms of scarlet. When Gina looked again, there was nothing: no trace of him at all, on the granite, or in the sea. No blood, no bubbles, no body. When she called out Josh's name, her voice was reedy again, lacking power and resonance. There came no answer but the shoosh of the waves, gone back to calm and placid, sparkling with scatters of sunlight.

A low moan escaped her. What had happened? Had Josh gone mad and jumped off the cliff? Or had it been no more than a terrible accident? She stared upwards again, willing him to be there. Was it better to be mad or to have witnessed a bizarre death?

How long she stood there, gazing between the sea and sky, between hope and reality, Gina did not know, but little by little, reality won out. At last, she had to admit what she had seen: her boyfriend falling to his inexplicable death, leaving her marooned here on the cliff face.

'Pull yourself together,' she told herself. 'You can't afford to panic.'

Was it her voice? Had she spoken aloud? Gina shook her head, took deep breaths, closed her eyes. She was not going to die here. She was not.

She opened her eyes and assessed the remaining metres of the route above her. No way she could solo out: some of those moves were too hard for her even on a tight rope. Breathe. Perhaps, if she pulled the rope back up, she could abseil off the camming device that was holding her in place. She touched the chill metal shank, tugged at it to make sure it was secure, added a gated carabiner from which to abseil. It would do. It would have to.

It took her several minutes to haul the rope up from the platform, looping it over her leg to stop it tangling. Soaked by the waves, it was twice its usual weight, and the salt from the seawater stung her cuts and her arms ached. With trembling fingers, she worked her abseil device off the harness and tried to pay the wet rope through it. Cold and shocked, she was finding it far too hard. When she pushed harder, the abseil device shot out of her grasp and went spinning off into the void.

Gina let out a sob as it hit the rocks below with a clink. Now what? Tears began to sting her eyes.

You are not going to die here, the voice reminded her. *No tears: women are strong.*

And suddenly her head was clear. She was not going to die: she was *not*. With extreme care, she drew her pack around to the front so she could get her phone out. It still had charge: even more miraculously, it had signal.

She punched in 999 and asked for the coastguard.

Half an hour later, the local rescue team arrived above, and an orange RNLI inshore lifeboat came right into the zawn. The rescue team set up their ropes and a cheerfully brisk woman abseiled down to where Gina stood, shaking, on her makeshift belay. Within minutes, she had roped Gina into the system and was lowering her down to the wavecut platform, where the RNLI team awaited.

Was it the shock of all that had happened, or the relief of being rescued that came over her then? Gina would often ask herself that question in the years to come, for the events of that day would continue to haunt her, even when she was happily married to Ed, with three kids, running her own highly profitable company. For, as she was lowered past the crack leading into the cave, she was absolutely, definitely, sure that she saw a figure standing there: a tall, red-haired woman, wrapped in a weird green light that struck the twisted golden torc around her neck – a queen, a tribal chief. And, as their eyes had met, the queen's lips had curved into a knowing smile, as if sharing with Gina the secrets of the Black Zawn.

You are worth so much more.
Go out and take it.
For you, and for me.

The Todden

Emma Cowell

Cadgwith 1975

Few people in the village paid attention to Lady Eloise, save for the odd glance from an aged fisherman or occasional curtsy from her domestic help. 'Good morning,' they'd say, bobbing briefly and averting their gaze. Eloise could almost taste the silent hierarchy of class that inspired their deference, eyes compelled to fix on the ground as she passed. It wasn't only her breeding that conjured forced politeness. She had been deemed mad as a child, unhinged enough to be sent to the institution at Bodmin as a teenager before war had broken out. It was the county asylum to treat the clinically unstable. She'd stayed there for six years before emerging back into the outside world as a 21-year-old woman. The age when she should have been presented into London society, a husband identified, and her future mapped out. But Eloise was never permitted to provide an heir for fear she should pass on her afflictions.

Thirty years had passed since she was permitted home to Cadgwith from the hospital. So much was different in the Cove and, at the same time, it wasn't. Those she remembered from before her stay in the facility were marked with time and age, yet the headland provided the constant comfort of familiarity. But there was a hole in the heart of the village, a gaping space in her chest because Edmund Pascoe was gone. Everything seemed dull without him, like having lived for a time in Technicolor, then condemned to dwell within a grey-washed world. Eloise found she could hardly taste the coconut on her tongue from the sun-scorched gorse any more, nor smell the seaweed nestled amongst the piles of rotting fish guts which barely touched her nose.

Coming back to her home from the asylum in 1945 had been a covert operation under a cloak of secrecy with her mother at the helm of the mission. It was akin to a kidnapping but in reverse and the memory lunged forwards in her mind. Her heart had been filled with such hope that Edmund would still be waiting for her. A car had collected her in the dead of night to begin the long journey from Bodmin to the Lizard. There had been another war, she'd been told, but it was now over. Nobody had mentioned the conflict on the ward but, when she considered it, she recalled the hospital nights had latterly been punctuated with the feral groans of men which had dampened the manic screams of the female patients. She was begrudgingly brought home by her mother, the Dowager Duchess, because she was required on the estate to help Cook and tend the land because many of the men hadn't returned, lost in battle. She couldn't imagine what they'd been fighting for and wondered whether it had all been worth it. As the motor car had rattled across the roads, Eloise tried to suppress the resentment she felt towards her mother for sending her away. She'd been torn from her heart's true love without any good reason aside from being 'different'. Her mother's disappointment in her was plain, Eloise didn't fit the mould of a lady. Far from it, her mother thought her insane.

'Be warned, Eloise, one sniff of one of your episodes and you'll be back at Bodmin faster than you can run a comb through that bird's nest of yours.' Her mother had forced stray ringlets away beneath Eloise's headscarf as they'd bumped around in the noisy vehicle bound for home. Her fingers had chafed her skull, but Eloise hadn't flinched. It was the first human contact she'd had from a family member in six years, and she'd basked within the sadistic pleasure of it. The sound of the engine during the lengthy journey had lulled Eloise to slumber. A stringy line of drool tickled her chin, rousing her from drowsiness. She'd caught the look of disgust on her mother's face as she'd stirred.

When they'd finally reached the manor at St Ruan, she was firmly ensconced in an eaves room, impounded between the four walls from dawn until dusk never to be seen in plain sight by anybody outside the estate. She was only allowed out at night, limited to the dark winding roads from Grade Church towards the sea beneath the moonbeams that illuminated her pallid colouring. As a reward for docile behaviours, she was occasionally granted leave from the attic for the kitchen. There she'd watch the giant backside of the cook bustling from stove to the butcher's block and back again. Her unsubtle mutterings just above the point of hearing consisted of diatribes about madness and witchcraft; her barbs were as thick and weighty as the white sauces she made. Eloise would quietly observe the rotund woman stir bubbling pots, greedily helping herself to the contents. Even though food had still been rationed at the time of her release, the effects of the war had lingered both seen and unseen. If Eloise made any sound, even a tiny coo at the fluffy cluster of fireside kittens, she'd receive a smack to the back of her head with a wooden spoon. Were Eloise more belligerent and entitled, she would have threatened Cook's dismissal. But she found herself enjoying the harsh acknowledgement. Besides, she'd become accustomed to punishment. It was a masochistic method of communication with which she was familiar, and it brought a strange, albeit painful contentment. But Eloise would dutifully sit, passively whiling away the time until the sun set. Then she would rove the village.

Even now after all this time, she still walked each day after dusk, finding it gave her something to look forward to. In her mind's eye, she heard the church bells mark the small hours, though the bell tower now sat empty like a barren womb. Exploring the village under the cover of night remained her favourite thing to do, and she continued to trample the well-trodden paths these thirty years later. It felt like Cadgwith was hers as she reclaimed Cornwall through the darkness. Nobody could take it away from her. Those lonely night-time assignments decades ago were supposed to have been her penance, a condition of her release from Bodmin, but she found she preferred the pitch dark to the day – the company of sprites that loitered in the shadows and the kindly ghouls that soared within the wind were favourable in comparison to her family or the staff. She felt in charge of her destiny, as opposed to the strict regime that had been forced upon her in the daytime at her mother's command – banished to her room in solitary confinement.

The one place she never set foot at any hour then or now was The Todden. It was a small cliff set between the two beaches in the heart of the Cove, an outcrop of rocks that extended like a stony muscular limb into the water. It made her shiver, so she set her course deliberately to evade it.

When walking at night as the memory of the Grade Church bells echoed four of the morning, she would glide towards Lethe Place, the house where Edmund Pascoe had lived. He was her childhood friend and confidante who hadn't scoffed at her wild ideas or emotional responses to nature. He'd listened to her, entertained her notions and personal beliefs that spirits lived within a bird's song, or hid beneath the clouds that hung above the misty autumn horizon. Ghosts, she knew, were swirling all around. The dead never truly left their home. He hadn't thought her ideas insane. Her teenage heart had shattered to be parted from Edmund, like she'd been ripped away from the other half of her soul. The single memory she cherished, and still clung to, was the feel of his warm lips on hers as they'd lain amongst the wildflowers in a distant field on her family estate. But he was gone. No matter how hard she looked, she couldn't find him and nobody she asked knew where he was. She'd lost her one true love, and it was entirely her mother's fault.

Eloise spent her days drifting happily around Cadgwith Cove – walking was a pastime of ladies, she knew, along with needlepoint and reading. No other pursuit aside from her rambles gave her joy, which was fortunate because there was little else left for her to revel in. Not since Edmund had disappeared. She was afraid the war had claimed him, though nobody could confirm it. There was no evidence in the graveyard, and none of his kin remained, but Eloise refused to give up her search.

As she strolled from the top of Prazegooth down towards the wooden stick in the pit of the village, she yearned for a kind word with somebody. Anybody. Usually, she would sit beside the gnarly old fishermen taking a break from mending their nets. They'd exchange pleasantries but nothing more substantial. She couldn't recall the last meaningful conversation she'd had with a neighbour, but Eloise was happy with her own company – she'd become accustomed to the silence as the years had passed. The animals on the estate where she lived in St Ruan paid her more mind than those who resided in the parish. Chickens clucked in a temporary frenzy when she approached to collect their eggs, cows mooed at her between bites of sweet silage, and horses stamped their hooves, tossing their glossy chestnut manes at her presence.

But that July morning, she happened upon her favourite fisherman, Mr Jowan. He rose slowly to his feet sweeping withy branches aside to make room for her, then allowed Eloise to sit first before returning to his labour,

''Tis an easterly, ma'am. They say when the wind is in the east, the fish'll bite the least, so us don't launch they boats,' ventured Jowan with a twinkle of his cornflower-blue eyes. He was holding a clutch of willow stems that he used to patch up his lobster pots.

'And when the wind is in the west, the fish bite the best... I believe that is correct Mr Jowan, is it not?' responded Eloise with a wry smile.

He chuckled a husky rasp, before setting his sticks aside to open his tobacco tin. Its lid was painted with an oil depiction of a crabbing boat traversing the seas. Eloise picked it up for closer inspection.

'It's beautiful. One of yours?' she asked as her thumb brushed the lumps of paint that made up the churning water in the scene; cobalt blue merged with turquoise, flecked with thick clumps of white. Her head began to spin slightly at the collision of colour, and she set it down.

Jowan nodded. 'You have a good eye, ma'am, and yes, 'tis one of mine. I can only paint them crabbers going in one direction – headed for 'ome. That's how you know 'tis one I done.'

Lady Eloise inhaled the salty air to steady her nerves. 'I don't suppose there is any news of Edmund Pascoe. I know I always ask, but what does one have if not hope?'

Jowan sadly shook his head, 'I'm afraid not, ma'am. And I suggest you prepare yourself for the fact he may never return to the Cove. Not now after so long.'

He smiled kindly, indulging the identical conversation they'd repeatedly had, but a shiver rippled along her bony spine. Despite the melancholy suggestion of Edmund's demise, which she refused to believe, the conversation had heightened her blood making it run faster with the joy of connection. Most were afraid to speak to her, but not Mr Jowan. Eloise's 'ailment' sent most fleeing for cover rather than encounter her.

She left Mr Jowan to his toil and began to walk up the hill. Days were long and carefree for Eloise in her tiny corner of Cornwall, almost as if time had stood still. It remained rich in tradition, although the purity of its history had been somewhat blighted by the outsiders who had started to buy the old cottages, making their mark and claiming the Cove for themselves. It was becoming a sideshow, like one would find on the edge of a pier, as spectators came to stare at the freakish wonder of Cornish life. The authenticity of the place was slowly being eroded just as the tide stealthily claimed the land for itself, gobbling away with its watery jaw. She hardly recognised anyone who lived there, few of her people remained and her mother was now dead, though for that she was grateful. Their relationship had been strained to say the very least. The Dowager Duchess Bligh had cruelly preferred Lady Eloise firmly out of sight and her daughter was more than happy to comply. But now she was free of her mother's grasp and was Lady of the Manor in her own right.

As she reached the brow of the hill, she turned to look behind her. The view of the thatched cottages that huddled together afore the sea warmed her empty heart as her precious Cove extended into the cliffside – almost as if the houses had always been there and were growing out of the rock. She ran down the makeshift stone steps towards 'Little Beach', avoiding The Todden. It still felt like a novelty, a forbidden treat to sit on the pebbles in daylight, sifting stones through her fingers. She was no longer a dirty secret to be kept hidden, risking a stain on her family's good name in case daylight ignited her passions. She was head of the clan now and answered to no one. Eloise was enjoying the kiss of sunshine on her skin making it glow brightly in the crisp morning light.

Eloise eventually walked away from the sea up towards St Ruan, loitering on the way upon the bridge. She distracted herself by tossing sticks over the barrier then running to the opposite side, craning her neck to see if her twig appeared. Hours seemed to pass repeating the same action, dashing across the road and back again, though she was alert for anyone who could give her silly mischief away. It wouldn't do for a person of her breeding to be seen indulging in such childish pastimes. When a stranger neared, Lady Eloise hid within the thickets above the stream and hissed at them through the branches while bulrushes tickled her ankles. She enjoyed watching people start, then desperately survey their surroundings for the source of the noise. They called it 'the haunted bridge' which made press her palm hard against her mouth to muffle her giggles. There were no spirits, only her. Eloise knew how to avoid detection, suppressing her laughter at the whitening of their skin, gooseflesh visibly rising on their arms. She was amused by their superstitious stupidity, convinced every corner of Cornwall was riddled with ghosts.

The next day, she headed for the Cove as usual and sat on the stick – the thick slab of driftwood slung between two stone pillars within a wall. She was disappointed that Mr Jowan wasn't there, but she entertained herself by observing the to-ing and fro-ing of the outsiders who were now residents. Some of the *emmets* even dressed in a costume that they though befitted a Cornish village, like they were acting out a part: fisherman's smocks, Breton striped shirts, and clumsily-rolled cigarettes with contraband tobacco bought from a man beneath the pavilion in the park. They stored it in the painted tins that Mr Jowan sold for beer money, though Eloise had heard him joke that, in the summer months, he never needed to buy a pint of ale. He could spin such a wonderfully embellished yarn to entrance the holidaymakers who encountered him. She'd always wondered whether Mr Jowan had come from the sea, born of a mermaid perhaps. His irises were coloured like the lapping waves that surrounded the isle of Tresco.

The water had been a magnet for Eloise ever since she could

remember. She was lured by an imaginary siren song, pulling her towards its grey murky depths. It was a place of burgeoning beginnings and inevitable conclusion; where fishes were given life, then netted to their death to provide the bounty of nourishment for those who feasted upon their flesh and bones. The cruel and relentless circle of life fascinated Eloise with its callous turns.

After a long blissful day whiled away in the heart of the Cove, Eloise walked her trail back towards the farmyard at the mouth of the estate. Lifting her pale skirts, she managed to avoid the piles of animal excrement that littered the yard. Someone should have swept the pathway, she thought, knowing she ought to take a firmer hand with her staff. The sunset was enveloping the world in a peach-tinted embrace. Even the cows on the hillside looked changed from the touch of fading beams. The Friesians seemed painted with gold; their former white crisp base coats were softened by the dying embers of the summer sun on its final descent beyond the headland. As she stood and surveyed her homeland, she felt free but knew she was also trapped, like she was split in two. She was stuck in a cage made of her own longing for Edmund. It was pointless, he was gone, but yet still he plagued her thoughts, disturbing her mind throughout the days and nights. Where was he? He had to be somewhere near; she could feel his heart's breath in the air. She was determined to hunt down the source of her turmoil, to discover once and for all what had happened to her beloved. As dusk began to extend its creeping tendrils across the pastures, she strode back across Ruan bridge with no mind for the dawdling folks leant over the guard rail to view the rushing water below.

'Ha!' she shouted for fun as she passed, darting into the hedgerow. They gave a cursory jump, but they didn't see she was the source. Instead, they looked up to the boughs of the trees which were creaking and rattling in the wind, the leaves like castanets, clacking the rhythm of a Cornish breeze. A small boy met Eloise's eye as she glanced over her shoulder at him. She winked and he giggled, galloping after her, before his arm was caught by his father and he was pulled backwards, his spirit curtailed. Their dog whimpered and backtracked on its hind legs and Eloise sneered in jest. Its high-pitched whining was scolded away by its owner. Eloise continued to pound the winding lanes above Cadgwith Cove, doggedly set on seeking out news of Edmund.

'He hasn't been seen here for a long time, a very long time,' was as helpful a clue as she received. She ought to prepare herself for the fact he was never coming back for her, but she simply refused to let him go. He wouldn't leave her, she knew it in her bones, she would never give up her search for him.

Eventually having exhausted every avenue and off-shoot of the lanes and roads leading to the Cove, Eloise was spent. She entered the inn to hear the shanties of old being sung by those who had no connection to the heritage of the songs. Strangers claiming the Cornish anthem of Trelawny as theirs, raising their glasses in celebratory cheers. Yet with each clink of their drink, Eloise retreated backwards and through the stable door in horror; she felt like she was losing her home.

She no longer recognised the spaces that had once been the setting for her childhood fancies or the places of refuge to hide from judgment. The languid days she'd spent when she was little with the horses tethered outside the public house, sitting beneath their flanks out of sight. The sweet stench of muck, kelp, and ozone combined to create a scent that was uniquely Cadgwith.

Yet it was being extracted from her grasp, it smelled like a foreign body, a stranger. Others were pulling it away from her and she felt afraid.

As Eloise withdrew from the alehouse, there was only one place left to search for Edmund, and it was the only place she couldn't bear to go: The Todden.

Mr Jowan's woven withy lobster pots were piled high on the concourse. Her fingers traced the spines of the branches within the mesh, some discoloured by the salty sea and others bent in deference to the current that had smashed their frames against the impenetrable rocks. Even the sea seemed quieter despite its relentless thumping on the shingled shore. Since she'd been parted from Edmund, the world was less in every way.

She took a step onto the green verge. At the start of The Todden, there were cottages at either side. Her eyes traced the large white thatch to the left and its smaller identical relative to her right. Her shaky foot reached out to extend into another footprint that would leave no mark, such was the spongy grass that coated the granite. She looked down at her black velvet shoes. They were splattered with mud and fronds of seaweed had draped across the almond-shaped toes. They must be rotten through, she thought to herself. She picked up her white skirts in an attempt at decorum and to avoid her lady's maid's expression should she tar them further. Then, she dropped them back to the floor. What did any of it matter anymore? Propriety counted for nothing.

The wind whipped at her long blonde hair and the sea swirled grey and dark, white foam splattered the rocks and bubbled on the surface like a boiling cauldron. She looked back across the village. The Cove was being lost to those outsiders who would grind away its provenance. It was filled with pretenders. Locals were all crumbling beneath a new budding history which would rise from what was wrecked. She wanted no part of it, not if she couldn't share it with her true love.

As she stepped forwards, her body took on a purpose, quelling the innate fear she felt. Her eyes lifted to the horizon, and her heart constricted with joy. There! She suddenly saw Edmund's silhouette ahead at the end of The Todden facing out to sea. His military uniform looked at odds with the seascape and she was unsure why he was wearing it. Perhaps his service was still required. The slight hunch of his right shoulder from a childhood case of polio marked him out clearly as the root of her heart's craving. She knew him better than her own face and he had been here, waiting, all along. She'd known it in her soul, he would never have left her. If only he had come for her, she wouldn't have wasted so much time.

'Edmund!' she cried, but her urgency was swallowed by the roaring sea as the tempest reached its climax. 'Edmund,' she tried again, but still he didn't turn. She gingerly stepped out further onto the cliff, the perilous drop either side made her legs wobble. His figure was beginning to fade until he was just vapour, and she ran toward it to clasp some of him in her fist, falling to her knees as she tried to grasp onto him. In that moment, she knew he was gone, it was the ghost of the man she had loved and always would. The mist that made up Edmund was swallowed by the storm and he was no longer there. She felt her heart crack open, the pain as acute as it had been when they were first separated. She could hardly stand as tears streamed down her face and she sobbed. She raised her head to the heavens and screamed his name into the whistling wind, vowing never to rest until she found him. The noise was akin a banshee's cry, and she felt the rocks beneath her feet vibrate. The boom of the waves thundering into the rocky abyss below spurred her onwards until she was teetering at the precipice like she was standing at the edge of the world. The urge to be gone was overwhelming – it consumed every cell in her body. If she couldn't have Edmund, she didn't want to live.

She held out her arms in front of her and frowned as seaweed began to appear on her wrists, coating her body like she had only just emerged from the sea but yet no water had touched her. The tangled fronds of kelp were like unwelcome bracelets, brown and shining over her translucent hue which was beginning to turn grey. Her limbs started to swell before her, bloating with cracked, open rotting sores. Layers of skin peeled away to reveal the bones beneath, flesh had been gorged upon by sea creatures, her knuckles naked and bloodless.

Eloise realised she had been here in this moment before. She was repeating her history, longing to plummet towards the depths of the unforgiving waters again, to dash out her brains once more upon the immovable rocks of history beneath. Her heart was brimming with an unfulfilled love, and her pain had nowhere to disperse.

As she stood and looked out at the smudge of a pencil line that made up the murky horizon, she tasted salt in her mouth and her hands travelled to her face. Her neck was swollen begging for air, the pressure behind her eyes was intolerable as dank murky seawater that had already filled her lungs thirty years ago resurfaced again, trickling down her dress, spewing from her mouth.

The memory of her demise returned. The Todden was the site of her soggy grave where she had chosen her own death. The swirling mass below was a vortex that had taken her life once and yet she was destined to repeat her path, never to live or die in peace while Edmund was out of her reach. Lady Eloise was condemned to fruitlessly haunt the tiny fishing village in search of her lost love for the rest of time.

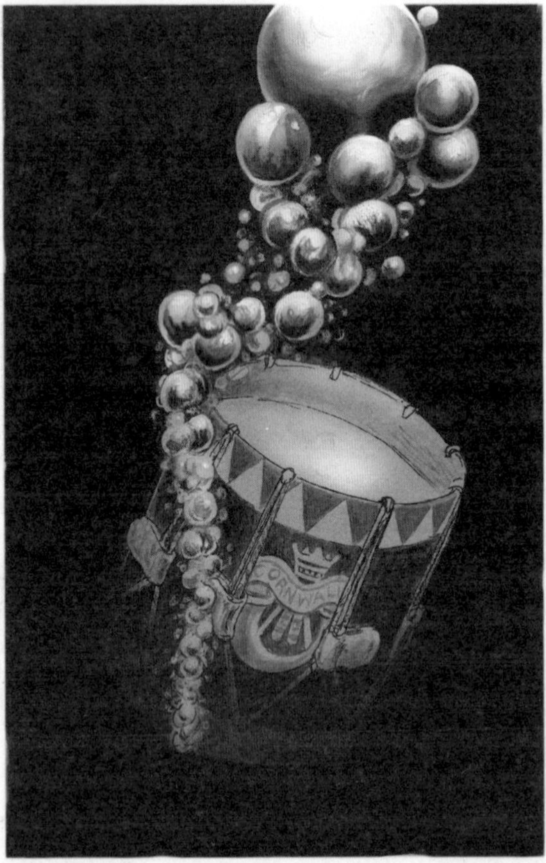

The Drummer Boy

Liz Fenwick

They are restless tonight, the dead. They call to me as the crescent moon rises. The sky is too clear while the ground is covered in a harsh frost. I shiver. My woollen shawl does little to protect on this bitter January night in the year of Our Lord 1809. I have lived too many years and yet too few. As I walk the cliff, I feel the dead jostle me. They want to speak but I do not want to listen. To my left, the moon throws its light on the dark restless sea. Somewhere distant a storm blows, but here only the swell reveals the turbulence from afar.

I rub my arms with stiff fingers. The north-east wind carries a warning. For the souls around me, the warning came too late or not at all. Men, women, children roam this cliff watching, waiting, and weary. I feel it. It pulls at the threads of my skirt and on the loose tendrils of my hair. If I stop moving, they hold me fast. These are the ones who are not buried in the churchyard like they of late since the law changed, no these are the ones laid to rest on these cliffs. Unmourned, unshriven, unconsecrated. These are the lost souls. No proper burial. Simply placed in the ground where the sea brought them. It has not discriminated. The young, the old, the rich, the poor. They all lie beneath the soil and rise and walk the coast path at night watching the sea, ever vigilant.

I, Sarah Bolitho, have often walked this path with them. I've been damned by this gift as my mother and grandmother before me. But, unlike them, I have no wish for it. It is a blessing that I have only borne sons. Yet I have lost all but one of them on foreign shores, and my husband no longer comes to me although I could still bear a child. My grandmother continued bringing babes forth till she was near fifty and the last one took her from this earth. Of her twelve children only my mother and my uncle reached maturity. My uncle has made his fortune which in turn helped me.

The sea breathes powerfully and exhales harshly onto the cove below like a man who has drunk too deeply of ale. Rising and falling with assurance. It will have its way and people will suffer.

Tonight, my husband is somewhere on this sea on his way back from the Peninsular War. Captain Benjamin Bolitho is a seasoned soldier but no longer young. I married up but he married well. He has never understood how precarious my position is. Having borne three sons, I should be safe but only my youngest and my husband stand between me and destitution. My mother and my uncle both long since departed this earth.

I pause my wandering and feel a tug on my skirt. My heart wants to see one of my boys there begging for my attention, but it is someone else's child. I press on along the cliff. I am not heartless but there's no solace that I can offer the child or the lonely man. It is the women that my heart hurts most for. They have not only lost their own lives but their children's too. To lose a child is to lose part of your soul. I know this too well. Only months have passed since the word of Peter's death had reached me. He is now buried in foreign soil far from me, but he is always in my heart.

There are no trees along this stretch of cliff to break the weather coming ashore. You have to head inland to find them and even they are bent and broken from the relentless wind. Tonight's gale is full of death. I could tell someone that in a few hours we would have more loss of life here along this coast that we had ever seen, but no one would believe me. I am not trusted for I am different.

In the distance a figure comes towards me and the souls at my side dissipate. It's old Luggan and he'll be up to no good. Maybe he'll be stealing someone's lobster pots but more like it will be something worse. He's tried using false lights to lead ships to their end. He is foolish since lights are used to warn of the peril. Only he would think they would lure the unwary. Nonetheless, when I've seen him at it, I've done my best to stop him.

The sea giveth and the sea taketh. Luggan has no right to try and bring a ship down for his own gain. If a boat loses its way on the treacherous rocks of The Manacles that are like a wild sea-beast's teeth, then it be God's will. When those rocks grab hold of a poor vessel, it is broken apart like kindling. The Manacles have chewed many a boat and provided good harvesting for folk. Taking what has come freely onto the shore is not thieving. It's surviving which, in some years, can be very hard. This year has been hard.

Luggan lopes. His right leg doesn't work so well after it was caught in the rock when he was up to no good. Serves him right but I wish it had stopped him.

'What are you doing 'ere Mistress Bolitho?'

'Could ask the same of you?' I counter, pulling my shawl closer.

'Just easing my old bones? Nothing more.' He casts me a side eye. 'Is that a light you're carrying?' He points at my waist where the keys to the house hang bulky.

I send him a harsh look. He doesn't have a lamp with him either. It may be that he keeps them stored about the coast. But in my very core, I don't think the ships that will go down tonight will be because of him. The dead cluster around me.

'Well, in the village they talk… talk about you always being on the cliffs when boats come amuck.' He steps closer and his breath stinks of stale ale and something worse, decay.

'They say you speak to the devil, and witchlike cast spells…'

I raise an eyebrow. I hear the dead and know when boats will meet their end, but I have no power, no spells, and no control. I am a woman who is at the mercy of the law and the feeble body I inhabit. However, the village makes up their minds about a person with little or no information or truth.

'What they say about you is worse and is true,' I whisper.

He is always the first on the beach to harvest a wreck. Never passing on the amount he should. Half of it by rights should go to the lord of the manor. The great man controls the wreck rights, and the people are supposed to wait a year and a day before harvesting. No one did. They all pay their share, but Luggan never did. He is a known layabout. It is a wonder he keeps a roof over his head, and he wouldn't except for his thieving and harvesting.

'Well, take you care Mistress Bolitho.' He glances around the deserted landscape. 'Never know who's about on these nights.' He marches past nearly knocking me off my feet and down the steep drop to the shingle cove below. I press on along the path only turning back when I am certain he is well away.

In the time that I have been walking, the moon has been covered by sparse clouds that are now thickening. Tonight, snow will fall and tomorrow we will wake to tears. I am powerless even though I may see these things. They do no good for I know not who will come to their deaths on The Manacles in the coming hours, only that they will. I scream into the wind and silence answers me.

The house is in darkness when I return. I half expect that menacing man to be waiting in the shadows. With fingers that I can barely feel, I light the lamp and go to the first floor. The view from the bay of windows on a fine day feels as if I could see France, but tonight my weary eyes can't see my garden. Before I settle into my chair on this bitter night, I put more coal on the fire then adjust myself so that I can look out to where I know the sea is. I dim my lamp and wait. My two servants will be well asleep and never notice their mistress's night-time watch.

With only the sound of the dull tick of the tall case clock counting the seconds, snow begins to fall. All is still as the wind drops. My thoughts visit the past when my house was full and my husband at my side. In the deafening quiet of the falling snow, I hear my sons' laughter and the continuous noise of their boisterous play. Rarely did this house know a peaceful moment except in the smallest hours of the morning like now. These days my home is full of nothing but silence, so I walk the coast path every night in darkness with the dead as my closest companions.

Woken by a sound, I leave my dreams of forgotten happiness. The fire is mere embers and I am not alone. The air about me is disturbed. I smell the sea, soap, and rum. My first thought is to that vile man Luggan. The clock below chimes the hour. Five tolls. The door opens. I grab the fire iron.

A tall straight figure stands in the doorway. The dull fire casts little light. My shoulders drop as recognition hits and the iron in my hand clatters to the floor.

'Mother,' he says.

My youngest boy, Johnnie, with his lopsided grin and deep brown eyes comes towards me. I adjust the wick in my lamp. But what I see can't be true. His last letter just over a month ago said his return to Spain was imminent. He also told me he was in love and didn't want to go. When he wrote those words, his brother Peter had still been alive. All my men have sought glory in the service of the King and thus far Peter and Martin have fallen. But as I look at the man-boy in front of me I know I have lost all my sons. My legs wobble beneath me.

'Mother, we haven't much time.' He steps closer and I reach out. The dead who walked the cliffs I feel, therefore I should be able to touch my son. His hand takes mine. It is cold, colder than the gold of his signet ring glistening on his finger.

I swallow.

'Now is not the time,' he says, lifting my chin. 'I need you to help me, to do something for me.'

I close my eyes. This is the ghost of my last-born. Surely God would not torment me so?

'Look at me,' he whispers. 'I need you to understand.'

I obey him.

'Father is dead.'

As he says the words, I know them true.

'His ship went down an hour before mine. He was on his way home.' He takes my hand. 'Gather blankets and your best spade.'

I shake my head. This makes no sense.

'Do as I ask mother, we haven't much time and I will explain as we go.'

I tighten my shawl, gather the woollen blankets from my room, and the spade by the kitchen door.

'Johnnie?' I ask as snow covers my damp cheeks. The ground is white and hard and unforgiving as I try to keep up with him.

'Mother, there is a boy of seventeen – the drummer boy I wrote to you about.'

'The one you were teaching?'

'Yes, that one.'

'Thomas is alive, and you will pull him from the sea.'

The words 'save a stranger from the sea, he'll turn your enemy' race through my thoughts.

'You must save him and convince all he is me.'

I look at my boy beside me who is now more man than when he left three years ago at six and ten. How could I, even if I wanted to, convince them that a boy of seven and ten is a young officer?

'You must mother, for you.'

I stop walking.

'Father is dead, my brothers are dead, the house and the land will go to my cousin.' He urges me on. 'You will lose everything.'

His words are true. I came into the marriage with nothing. Lately the cousin has been sniffing around the farm and the house thinking that there could be money made. He thought there might be tin, or copper or stone worth taking from the ground. He will strip it all. The land calls out to me. My heart warns me of the peril ahead.

We reach the cliff, and the dead keep their distance, waiting. But Johnnie wouldn't be joining them. He'd be proper buried at the church as the law now requires. All those washed ashore must be buried in consecrated ground unlike these poor restless souls. There I could visit with him and know his bones were at peace.

The snow has ceased, and the wind has turned. It comes now from the south-east. The dark deep sea holds the dead in icy fingers. I feel them moving towards me with the tide.

'There is another reason you must save him and call him by my name.'

I frown.

'I told you I was in love.'

My heart leaps.

'She is my wife. We married six days ago.' He pauses. 'I received permission to marry from my captain as she is carrying my child.'

A child, a blessing.

'She is on her way to you. Thomas, the drummer boy, knows her and he will understand.'

Johnnie places his hands on my arms and looks directly into my eyes, pleading. 'Will you do this mother?'

I could not deny him this. 'I will.'

He points to the water. Barely visible, something floats on the surface. The sea is doing its best to bring it to the shore. The many dead watch and wait while I make my way down to an outcrop. My boys would fish from here. It does not take much to picture the three of them larking about together, jostling each other until one is in the water and sure to come home to me sodden wet. My breath catches. Johnnie will be the one this time, this last time.

The object in the water moves nearer the shore. The tide pushes it closer still and two bodies are on a piece of wood. Neither looks alive. I pick my way down to the exposed cove and wade into the sea. Icy fingers of weed wrap around my legs but I push on. I have gone beyond cold as I wait for the next wave to bring the bodies within reach.

Johnnie stands on the rocks, and I feel him willing me on. I must do this but how am I to convince those that knew him that this drummer boy is my son, my heart? And what of his wife, would she agree? She must, for if she carries a girl it won't protect us. The house will still go to my husband's cousin. Widow Tonkin lives by what scraps the village can spare. My future lies this way if this doesn't work and if Johnnie's wife is carrying a girl.

As the tide brings them closer, I don't know which is my son. Both are dark-haired but soon it is clear. I pull the plank close and work as swiftly as I can to bring the drummer boy onto the beach. He is alive, just. I wrap him in the blankets and wade back in. My heart is heavy as I cradle Johnnie's body close to me. Despite having talked with him, I had hoped it had just been a dream and I would find him alive.

His wet uniform doubles his weight but I manage to bring him beside the boy, who has the look of Johnnie. It startles me, the likeness does.

'I tried to… to,'

'Save your energy Thomas, you'll be needing it to stay alive.'

His eyes open wide at the sound of his name. 'Johnnie told me.' I look up to my son and not the cold body on the beach.

'Mother, you'll need to swap our clothes.'

I shake my head. I couldn't strip my son bare of all that he earned and had wanted.

'Tis only clothes mother.'

I sigh.

'Mistress, let me help.'

I look at him, truly look at him. He has kind clever eyes. They are not my Johnnie's, but he belongs to a mother somewhere.

'I have to ask you to become my son Johnnie Bolitho.'

He stares.

'I can't tell you how or why but I do.' I draw a breath and see the dead watching me. Johnnie is watching me. They have moved closer to him.

The boy shakes his head. 'I can't.'

'You can. His wife is carrying his child and she will need you and I will need you.'

'The ar… my.'

'We'll sort that,' I say not knowing how we would, and all the while Johnnie stands with his hand on my shoulder. 'We need to get you into his uniform.' I lean down and brush a piece of bladderwrack from Johnnie's white cheek, then slip the ring off his finger and place it onto the drummer boy's shaking hand.

The buttons on the sodden uniform are difficult but eventually my child lies as bare as he had come into the world. The uniform is not too ill-fitting on the drummer boy, and I didn't think he could shiver more. But his own clothes had begun to hold some warmth and he had just put on the clothes of a dead man.

'What do we do now?' he asks.

I don't know.

'Take me up and bury me just as the field ends,' Johnnie says.

I want to ask why but the drummer boy is already convinced I am mad.

'That way I can be near my love and see my child grow.'

I close my eyes and see my boys. That joy could be his but the pain too. To be so close but not be with them.

'I love this land as you do.'

The dead circle around him. I could do this. I must do this.

'Do you think you can help me carry him?' I ask.

The boy nods.

I lift Johnnie's head and shoulders while the drummer boy takes his feet.

'I tried to save him.'

'I know,' I say with what little breath I have. Dead bodies are heavy like their bones have turned to stone and their flesh to mud. Ashes to ashes. No burial with honour, no marking, no fine linen to cover his body.

Halfway to the spot the boy collapses. I settle my son's body and go to the beach to rescue the blankets and the spade along with the drummer boy's clothes. Once I have wrapped the boy in the blankets again, I pull my son up to the spot he wants. Time has passed and I know it will not be long before the sun rises. I must find the strength to do this.

Hidden from the path by a long-fallen boulder I begin to dig. The ground is as solid as the law I am breaking in doing this. He should be buried in consecrated ground with proper rites and honours. If I am discovered, I don't know what fate I will face but I can't dwell on it. There is too much at risk.

The work is slow and, when I have barely broken through the topsoil in a shape large enough to fit my son, I hear the footsteps. The bastard Luggan will see, and this plan will all fail. There would be nothing for Johnnie's wife and child. The drummer boy would be flogged for impersonating an officer and stealing his goods. God knows what would become of me.

'Ah, Mistress Bolitho, up to witchy things, I see.'

He stinks of brandy. No doubt French brandy that he's not shared out and which he most likely kept hidden on our land.

'Killing and hiding the evidence.'

The drummer boy is out of sight just down below. I need him to stay there. This man is slippery and would strike like a conger eel in any way he could.

The dead and Johnnie move closer to me. I need to act, and I need to do exactly what he accuses me of. I need to kill him. The shovel is awkward in my hands as he steps closer.

'You know you're a fine-looking woman.'

I don't reply.

'If you make me happy, I could forget what I've seen.'

The dead surround him with Johnnie at their front.

'What have you seen?' I ask.

'A fine woman with a dead man, a naked dead man.' He leers with a bit of spittle dribbling down his chin. 'One I s'pect she killed.'

I hear a rustle and I know that the drummer boy is about to try and intervene. I lunge forward ready to take the spade to his head. He takes a sidestep, guessing what I'm about to do. He comes at me, but he misses and goes over the edge. I hear his groan and the thud of his skull hitting the rock. The dead come tight to my side and together we peer over the cliff. I don't need to worry if he's alive as half his head is open. If he isn't dead yet, then he will be soon.

On the horizon the sky is brightening and I'm not making much progress, but I must bury my boy. I've managed maybe a foot into the ground, but my strength has left. The spade falls from my hands but it doesn't hit the ground. I look to see if the drummer boy has picked it up but it's the dead. A big ox of a man has taken over the task.

'Mother, they will do it.'

I shake my head, not understanding.

'You and yours have kept them company and now I will walk with them.'

I close my eyes. I feel his cold hand on my cheek. 'Remember, I will be here with you.'

I should be happy with this knowledge but I'm not.

'Now go. Take your son home. He will need all your strength and so will his wife and child.'

I swallow, wanting to speak but the drummer boy is beside me. He's watching the grave getting bigger but he can't see how. He looks from me to the grave. I place my hand on his head. 'You have a fever,' I lie.

'Go swiftly mother.' Johnnie takes my other hand for a moment. 'I love you.' He releases my hand and I look over my shoulder. They are lowering his body into the ground. Rays of sunlight break through the clouds warming the snow to gold.

The house appears with smoke rising from her chimneys. Home, home for now at least. The hard work to keep it is still ahead. But first to tend to this poor boy. His body shakes and a cough has begun.

My maid stands still like she has seen a ghost. She can't take her eyes from the boy at my side.

'Tis Johnnie and he needs a bath and clean bed and hot soup.'

The maid doesn't speak but scurries away while I lead the boy to the fire and wrap him in more blankets. I must make this convincing. The maid was only a girl when Johnnie left, but the cook will be more of problem. But she wouldn't go against me. I must think of only one trouble at a time and the biggest might just be keeping this young man alive.

The cook arrives bearing a steaming bowl of soup. She looks from me in my wet clothes and to the boy by the fire. I know not what she thinks.

'Mistress, go and change. I'll look after Master Johnnie.' Her glance darts from me to the boy. His hand is just visible and the gold of the ring glistens in the light of the fire.

'Shall I send for the doctor?' she asks as I reach the door.

'He'll be busy with the others,' I say, knowing that would be true enough.

I must notify the authorities. Prepare for Johnnie's wife, then I could return to the cliff and grieve both my husband and my son. For official word of my husband's death would come before the day is out. Bad news is like that.

The sun has set and the sky is a delicate pink as I walk towards the edge with small hands in mine. Their mother, Johnnie's wife, is visiting in the village. Twilight has fallen and this is the first chance I dare to bring them since the twins could walk and talk.

The dead are waiting. Johnnie stands towards the back as my grandchildren and I make our way. The souls clear the space around Johnnie. He doesn't move and I watch his daughter. She can't take her eyes from him. My grandson stares out to the darkening sky. He doesn't have the gift.

Johnnie bends low and Charlotte takes his hand. With eyes full of tears, he looks at her and then his son.

'Lottie, what's in your hand?' my grandson asks.

Charlotte looks from her brother to her father to me. She pulls her father towards her brother. She places her brother's hand on her father's and then puts her own on top.

'Granma,' she beckons me, placing my hand on hers, binding us together. 'Love... love is in my hand,' she says.

Johnnie tightens his hold. 'Love it is.'

'I hear a voice but it's not you Lottie and it's not Granma.' He looks to the space between us, unseeing.

'It's the voice of love,' I say, swallowing the tears. Love doesn't end.

The dead step closer.

Author's Note

In the early hours of 22 January 1809 two troop ships were wrecked on The Manacles during a winter gale. The first to go down was the transport vessel *Dispatch* at around four in the morning on the way back from the Peninsular War in Spain. There were seven survivors. An hour later HMS *Primrose*, an 18-gun brig sloop carrying troops out to the war, went down. There was one survivor, the drummer boy, who was saved by the fishermen of Porthallow.

A year earlier, in 1808, after the wreck of the HMS *Anson* near Loe Bar, Helston, local solicitor Thomas Grylls petitioned for the law to be changed so that the dead washed ashore would be given a proper burial in consecrated ground. This was known as the Drowned Persons Burial Act of the Grylls Law. Up until this change in the law, the bodies from shipwrecks were buried close to where they came ashore, without shroud or coffin. There is a memorial to those lost from HMS *Anson* on the path above Loe Bar.

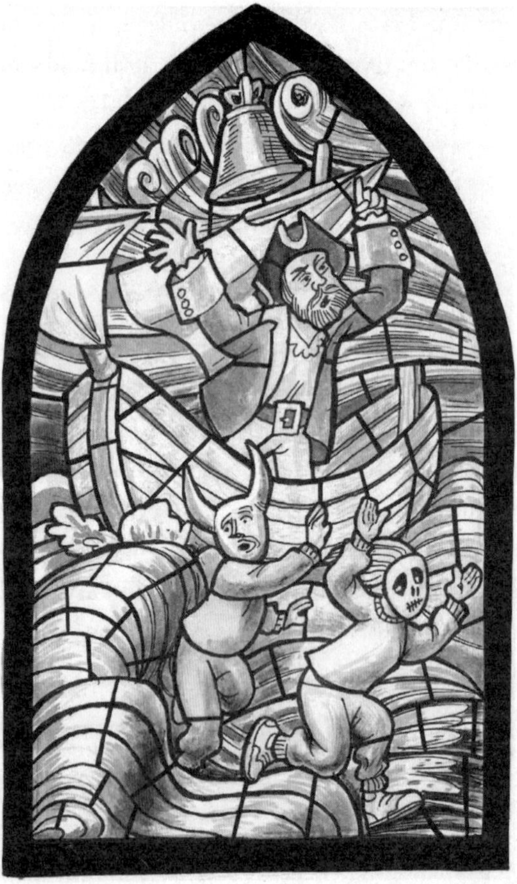

The Storm Bells

Pauline Sheppard

It is said to be an ill omen if a bell rings for no apparent reason. So when the Number 5 down St Gluvias Church went off just before tea on the 31st October, and there was no one in the belfry at the time, more than a few Penryn residents locked their doors, drew their curtains, and sat in their cottages to wait for bad luck.

Lucy's Aunty May did. Aunty May was a prodigious and literal reader of the Old Testament. She knew that devils walked the earth. Lucy, who was staying with her aunt for the weekend while her mum was on a course, knew that with the bolting of Aunty May's door, her Hallowe'en sleepover at Jimmy Nick's was suddenly and irrevocably cancelled.

'But, Aunty, it's been planned for weeks! Mum knows about it.'

'Way I see it, that bell was a warnin'. I don't hold with all that American treaty tricky malarkey. Now, you can either watch television with me... There's a nice documentary on about Bible stories as portrayed in stained glass – or you can go to bed.'

Lucy went to bed. She didn't know anything about stained glass and Aunty May didn't know anything about smartphones.

It is said that if two bells ring in a house at the same time, somebody is shortly going to leave. As Lucy's mum rang her sister on the landline to see how things were going, the digital bell of Lucy's smartphone rang upstairs, and Jimmy Nick made arrangements to spring his friend from captivity.

Just after midnight, while Aunty May dreamed of fiery red and blue stained-glass devils, Lucy crept out of her bedroom window.

Jimmy Nick was waiting in his dad's garage. He had the costumes ready. His was a red devil mask with enormous horns made of paper-covered withies, 'They idden so heavy as mashie paper,' he said. 'An' I still got these old black jeans an' jumper see? 'Ere's the skellington.'

Lucy pulled the skeleton mask over her face. The mask was glued to a woollen balaclava. It was itchy and it was hard to breathe without swallowing bits of wool.

'I got *the rest* 'ere,' whispered Jimmy.

The rest was two bags of flour and two cartons of sinister-looking red slime, 'Made'n with porridge an' ketchup,' he said, 'looks like sick, dunna? What we do is, we chuck this an' the flour at the door. Then we run like f... fury.'

'Where we meetin' the others?' asked Lucy.

'Graveyard 'course. You idden scared of old Cap'n Martin are 'ee? Him as was shipwrecked? Cos most girls are.'

'Course I idden.'

Jimmy spat into his slime.

'Spit or die,' he said.

Lucy spat.

Upper Market Street was strangely quiet as the devil and the skeleton walked side by side towards the clock tower. They saw no one, apart from a special constable who followed them until she stopped to chat to a couple of ghosts having a fag outside the door of the Seven Stars.

'That bell's put the wind up the whole town,' said Jimmy. 'Full moon too.'

They turned into St Gluvias Street.

'I ain't afeared though. Are you?' Jim swaggered.

'Now that Special's gone, we can start. Less do Deaf George.'

He took a handful of slime. 'Now, soon as it sticks, whack on the flour!' he ordered.

The porridge made a satisfactory splodgy sound on Deaf George's door and began to slip a glutinous trail down over the letter box.

The Devil hissed: 'Lucy! The Flour!'

Lucy threw the flour. At that moment there was a gun shot from the darkened cottage. Lucy gripped Jimmy's arm.

'Get off! S'only Deaf George watchin' *Die Hard 2*.'

'I knew that,' said Lucy.

Suddenly there was a sound of an explosion from inside the house.

'Thass the bit with the ejector seat,' said Jim.

To their horror, the door burst open and they were caught in the bright beam of a torch and held by a rasping, angry voice.

'Thass you Jimmy Nick ena? An' who's that you got with you! I'll have you! I will! I'll have you fer this!'

They ran into Commercial Road and didn't stop until they panted into Church Hill. Then they fell about, gasping and laughing. Jimmy did a war dance.

'See his face! 'Ere, 'ee idden so deaf after all isa! Silly old bugger. Can't frighten me! No one can't frighten me!'

They were dancing past the vicarage when the big grapefruit moon that had hovered over St Gluvias Church tower suddenly went out. A wind whisked Jimmy's withy horns over the hedge and into the graveyard. Jimmy clambered up and over. Lucy scrambled after him.

'Jimmy! Jimmy!' It was pitch black and big drops of rain plopped. 'Jim... where are you?'

'Oooooooooooooohhh!' hooted Jimmy in his best ghost voice.

'Stop messing about, I'm getting soaked!'

'Ooooooooooohhhhhh!' came the reply. Then one more sudden high-pitched cry, 'Ooooooo-oof' was cut off and silenced.

'Jim?... Jim!'

The rain lashed out of the darkness. Lucy tore the balaclava from her head. 'Jim! Jim!' The rain stung her face and the wind whipped the trees against her as she fought her way towards Jim's last cry. Thunder rolled out of the darkness and the next livid lightning flash hung in the air, illuminating the black outline of the church. Jimmy's mud-spattered face grinned over a gravestone.

'Went arse over tit on one of they graves got a little low wall, y'knaw.' He rubbed his knee ruefully. 'Wow, what weather! Proper devil weather!' He pranced about the gravestones with his ghostly utterances.

'Oooooohhhhhh, oooohhhh! Bet the others'll be too scared come out in this.'

Lightning once again gouged through the dark to hover like laughing jagged teeth around the entrance to the church. The great oak door creaked and then slowly swung wide open.

'C'mon,' said Jimmy, 'less get under cover.' He grabbed Lucy's hand. 'S'all right, wind's blown it open. Vicar can't have locked up proper.'

As the light went out and more thunder crashed, they ran into the porch.

They stood in the doorway. 'I 'aven' never seen no rain like this,' said Jimmy. 'Comin' in all directions at once.'

'Sounds like the sea roarin',' said Lucy. 'D'you think, d'you think it was the bell?'

'Don't be daft, superstition that is. Bells don't go off a'ringin' on their own. Tes a squall, I've heared Dad tell about squalls comin' out the sea from nowhere.'

'I... I think the ground's moving beneath me.'

Lucy steadied herself against the church noticeboard and stared down at her feet but saw only water lapping over her shoes. 'It's the sea! Jim, it is! It is the sea!'

The wave crashed down and lifted them like flotsam from the safety of the porch before spewing them onto the wooden boards of the deck. In the lightning they saw a great ship's mast reaching into the black clouds. At its base stood the dark outline of a Captain as he called out of the past and into the storm.

'Heaaaave tooooooo!... Heaaave tooooo!'

Then it was dark again and his voice came from the violent blackness.

'Reefs innnnnn! Reeefs Innnnnn!'

A flapping of giant bird wings joined the hullabaloo as sails flapped and spanked and ripped through the rain and spars crashed to the deck. It was a terrible sound, but not so terrible as the Captain's final order:

'Run with the Storm!' he cried. 'Run with the Storm!' But he was nowhere to be seen.

The howling of the wind became unbearable as Lucy and Jim huddled by the ship's wheel. The heavy wooden deck was splintering like matchwood and hailstones as big as apples spat at them out of the dark and broke in ice-cold shards across their sea-soaked backs. They opened their mouths to cry out and no sound came from them as the wind stole their cries.

Then, above the storm, a new sound crashed and tumbled and rang out across the wind. It was the sound of bells. Church bells, ringing peals. Louder and louder and louder came the bells until with a mighty angry jangling ear-rattling roar it seemed that the storm was sucked through the church door into the nave and towards the bell tower. Lucy and Jim clung to the font as the water hissed past them with a final hollow gurgling growl. Then all became silent.

Lucy and Jim lay on the granite floor without speaking. Their eyes wide with fear as heavy footsteps trod past them out of the nave, into the porch, and out of the church. Framed in the doorway, the tall figure of Captain Martin dissolved in the gentle moonlight which returned as swiftly as it had left. The smell of sea and salt lingered in the open doorway.

'Did... Did that just happen?' asked Jimmy.

'I don't believe in ghosts,' said Lucy through chattering teeth.

'You're shakin' though.'

'Yes, I'm cold.'

Jimmy helped her up.

'You ent even wet,' he said.

Lucy felt his sleeve. 'Nor you. Let's get out of here, Jim. I want to go home.'

'It's like it never happened,' said Jim as they walked out into the night.

'Reckon we should tell?' Lucy looked at Jimmy's wide eyes. It took only a second for him to consider.

'Not Never,' he said. 'They woulden b'lieve it. I don't b'lieve it, an' I saw it.'

Behind them the church door slammed shut. In the bright moonlight Jim and Lucy ran like f...fury down Church Hill.

In the graveyard, a mischievous wind played with a pair of devil's horns and flour blew in little puffs across the grass.

In the morning, the vicar found a strand of seaweed in the porch but, wisely, he said nothing of it. For he alone amongst the rest of the inhabitants of Penryn had heard the bells.

It is said that ringing of the church bells during a storm might distract the spirit of the storm from his work and cause bad weather to abate. Captain Martin, Bell Captain, Ship's Captain returns when he can to ring the bells at St Gluvias Church.

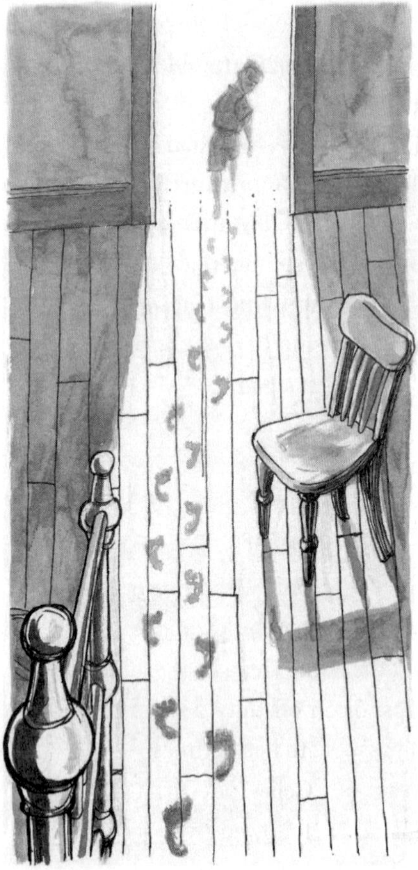

Celia

Graham Mitchell

The girl was neither here nor there. She lived life like she was floating in a feather bed, but she'd wake up someday on a hard wooden floor picking splinters out of her skinny backside. She remembered her father saying it clear as day sitting there waiting for his breakfast, her mother's aproned belly resting against the stove, bacon spitting in a pan.

The day the girl was born, her father wanted to name her Dot for an aunty who'd died of something internal during the first war, but her mother insisted on Celia after a song she belted out regular down the Hanley, a gutful of port and lemon for courage: 'Drink to me only with thine eyes, and I will pledge with mine.' She wanted better things for her daughter than blacking Rayburns, and the name Celia had a ring of something to it – an actress perhaps, or an off-duty duchess. A mother's gift, all she could offer, a passport to better times.

Twenty years on, Celia rode the tube Monday to Saturday to South Kensington followed by a short stroll to her work in Grayson's Emporium where they employed only fine-boned young ladies to walk the shop floor. Most days, the rattling journey passed in silence, save for an 'Excuse me' as she found a seat and thumbed her magazine, or applied make-up if she'd slept in, the train jolting her lips in her compact mirror. But today was not that kind of day. Today, time would slip like a scratch on a record.

A man opposite was practically taking the paint off her – men looked, they always did – and she let her eyes rest anywhere but on him. Monochrome ads for soap and boot black ran the length of the carriage but over the door was a poster advertising The Cornish Riviera – a chalky drawing of a train snaking past a cream-coloured beach. A woman with curly black hair was waist deep in the blue sea, a child beckoning to her in the waves and, in the foreground, a toothy, fresh-faced, young chap in a fisherman's smock. Another world far from busy station platforms and the squeal of tube-train brakes, and not for the likes of a Whitechapel girl, not then.

But four years later, there she was in a cottage garden on the edge of the Atlantic. Gulls wheeled high over the cliffs, and a moorland peppered with burial cairns came right down to the sea. Her mother was right, there would be no blacking Rayburns for Celia; she was meant for better things, at least until the wheels she set in motion that tube-train morning reached their inevitable end.

She met him at a holiday camp on the dunes overlooking St Ives Bay where she'd picked up a waitressing job. He asked her to dance but she couldn't when she was on duty, which he knew only too well, but he'd tried it on anyway. His toothy grin reminded her of someone, and it hit her that he was the spit of the toothy young fisherman on the tube-train advert, the absolute doppelganger. And when he told her that he fished for a living too, it seemed like the poster had somehow been made flesh.

Telfer was his name – it sounded almost foreign – but she said he could walk her home, and they spent the night tracing the maps of one another's bodies and were married within the year. As simple as that.

Herring had died out a decade since but there was plenty of mackerel, so he bought a ketch called *The General Gordon* and they rented a four-square house from Ewart Treloar who made his money farming eggs and bought hymn books for the chapel to guarantee his place in heaven. The chatter locally was that the marriage wouldn't last – that Telfer's head had been turned by this flighty London miss – so *The General Gordon* he renamed *Celia* and put to sea flying her knickers from the mast, and that put an end to it.

In '49 Grace came along, followed a year later by Archie, forcepsed into the world by the light of a kerosene lamp – electricity had yet to make it this far west. Telfer was a handsome man, hard-working too and, for Celia, life was as goosy as anyone had a right to expect it to be – until the April of '53 when summer came early for a few days and the thermometer down by the harbour read 86. That was when Archie drowned and, at a stroke, everything shifted, every ounce and inch of it.

Telfer buried their boy in a plot overlooking the sea, the wind whistling around the stones. He got through it all like a performance and was praised for his stoicism, but Celia, her heart not strong enough to stand public scrutiny, refused to leave the house. Instead, she locked herself away with Grace who fetched a box of crayons from the cupboard under the stairs and together they drew vast planets and moons and black starry skies with the same yellow-haired boy in every shape.

The doctor had given Celia sedatives, two to be taken before bed, but they just made her feel groggy. So, while Telfer slept, she sat in the bedroom window and watched the yellow of the gorse in the fading light and the granite sparkling in the hedgerows, until a deep darkness fell over the place as black as ink, then she lit a candle and went downstairs to make a drink, setting the kettle to boil on the stove.

Outside, the wind played around the house and, somewhere inside it, there rang a single solitary note, low and melancholy at first then rising through the registers until it rang high and true. She looked outside to try and locate the source of it, but there was nothing, just trees moving in the breeze and her candle-lit reflection in the window. Suddenly chilled, she closed the curtains and stepped back. And that was when she felt it – her bare feet on the wooden floor, a seeping, chilled-to-the-bone cold that rose up her body like she'd stepped into a wave. It was. It was water. She'd trodden in water. A puddle of it in a perfect circle on the kitchen floor, smooth-edged like mercury. Smaller drops led away across the room to the back door, and she held the candle close to the lock to check the key hadn't been turned, but the door and windows were all closed and secure.

She crouched by the puddle and rippled the surface, tasting it on her finger – salt like the sea. And now, as she watched, the water ran quickly away from her, melding into rough-edged ovoids that blurred to become digits – toes – feet – a child's footsteps, Archie's footsteps, stepping towards her from the back door.

She called out his name and searched the corners of the room; then outside, shielding the candle against the wind, she scanned the hedgerows, but there was no-one.

And when she turned back to the kitchen, all evidence of what she saw there on the floor – or thought she did – had already disappeared like mist in the sun.

Was it an aberration, a product of her grief when the night felt like it might never end? Since the boy died, she'd thought she'd seen and heard him everywhere, a glimpse of him running on the coast path, his voice in the night. Perhaps in her sorrow she projected him onto the places he'd once occupied. That's what she told herself – that people lived on in the consciousness of their loved ones, and that these last weeks the barrier between her mind and the rest of existence had smeared like the water on the kitchen floor.

She didn't mention what had happened that night to Telfer for fear he'd think she was losing her mind. For Celia, since Archie had died, time had lost its rhythm and become unanchored, but Telfer carried on as though little had changed. The truth was that she blamed herself for what had happened to the boy and, though he'd said nothing of the sort to her, she believed he blamed her too – how could he not?

She'd told herself that their life here was perfect but now it seemed to her that even the way they'd met was utterly fantastical. A poster on a tube train had set her imagination running so fast that she'd washed up here living a version of it. It was at once perfectly romantic yet utterly fanciful, like Cary Grant in Technicolor, but looking back on those early years together now, Celia convinced herself that she was living another woman's existence – that there was an element of perfection here that she'd simply imagined into life, whereas in reality she was ostracised and isolated. She was not of this place, but neither was she a Londoner any more and, in truth, when the sea was picked up and flung relentlessly at the house, she'd felt a craving in the pit of her stomach for busy streets and warm cafés, and a loneliness came over her like the tolling of a church bell.

What if she'd stayed in London and become a different version of herself than this country mother? Someone perhaps like her colleague at Grayson's who'd met a man with family money and opened her own boutique on the King's Road. That could have been Celia, couldn't it? Another Celia. She could have been that woman.

Was that the serpent in this Eden? This seam of dissatisfaction and ungratefulness? Was that why Archie died? Because when she was supposed to be here, fully here, she was actually dreaming of somewhere else?

The afternoon everything changed, the hot spring weather had brought shoals of mackerel closer to shore so Telfer was out fishing off Porth Ledden. Stretched out in the sun, Celia lay on the clover lawn in front of the house stripped to her bra to encourage a tan and dreaming of this other Celia, her shop shelves piled high with Chanel and Dior, her assistants welcoming customers, the Knightsbridge ladies in swaying hems, and girls-about-town with their wasp waists and pencil skirts. And all that time in the garden, Grace and Archie were running and playing, their voices melding with the tinkle of Celia's imaginary shop doorbell.

The children had started out happily enough together, but they'd fallen out over who should be first to ride the rusty tricycle. Grace withdrew in a tizzy and clambered fearlessly up into the branches of an oak tree too tall for Archie to follow, so the boy made do with a wooden water-butt Celia had intended to get a lid for, which was held together by metal hoops which doubled as perfect footholds.

It was the creeping quiet that alerted her, no more trill of children's voices, just the wind in the yellow gorse. She thought perhaps Archie had wondered up onto the coast path, so she went looking for him there, calling his name, her heart in her mouth.

Dusk had begun to fall when Telfer found him, the walnut swirl of the boy's hair as he floated face down, the barrel still full from the winter rains.

After the night when Archie's footsteps had appeared, Celia spent every waking moment watching for him to return but, for months, there'd been no sign, and she'd withdrawn further and further into herself. A summer storm had raged for almost a week trapping her and Telfer in the same four walls. He tried as best he could to reach out to her, but Archie's passing had put a bolster between them and, when the weather finally let up, he was glad to get away to sea, if only for a night.

Up at the house in the small hours, the windows were open wide, moonlight playing like an aura around the edges of the drawn curtains. It was humid, Grace was restless, and she'd padded through to her mother to be soothed and cuddled back to sleep. Celia hadn't slept either, not more than an hour or so in months – and only then when exhaustion overcame her. Now, she lay there rigid, listening. Perhaps if the wind had whipped around the house as it usually did then she wouldn't have noticed it. She raised herself up. It seemed to come from different sources outside, or perhaps it was something moving quickly there. A distant sound pitched high like a woman's voice, a wailing, a keening.

She pushed back the sheet and stood in the bedroom doorway. Moonlight silvered the landing, the window there uncurtained, and now a silence descended so deep she could hear the blood pumping in her veins.

A box of matches sat on the window ledge. She struck one, and the brief burst of flame picked out something glistening further along the landing. Drops of water had again collected on the varnished floorboards, but there on the landing this time closer to where she and Grace were sleeping. She held the match to bring the water into focus again and, just as before, it melded and ran and blurred into little footsteps.

A warm hand found hers. Grace. The girl had woken and seen her mother standing stock still on the landing listening. Celia shushed her and held her close. Oh dear God, she should have scooped her up and ran, but that keening was there with her so shrill and loud that instead she stood sentinel, the match's halo lighting the landing. Then she saw it in the far corner – just shadows at first – then, as it moved, the shape of a boy's face, a face she knew as intimately as her own, the mouth opening into a scream before the match sputtered and the shadows dissolved him.

The following morning, the sun had yet to rise when Telfer landed his catch of rainbow mackerel on the quay before climbing the coast path to the cottage where he hung up his oilskins and wandered through to the kitchen for an hour to himself and the paper. But the girls were already up, Grace chatting away nineteen to the dozen, bacon spitting in the pan. Celia too was animated, her movements quick and sharp, all angles and levers, and, for the first time in an age, her face opened into the broadest of smiles and his world seemed to have miraculously reset itself. Until he saw it. She'd laid four places for breakfast – two sets of steel cutlery for herself and for him, and two more made of faded yellow Bakelite for their children.

He bided his time until Grace left for school then framed himself to voice what he'd been silently rehearsing, but there was no need. Celia was straight out with it – she'd heard the boy in the night, she'd seen him.

He took her hands, but she wouldn't have it. She would not be spoken to like an invalid. She knows what she saw. What the hell could he say? It wasn't her fault what happened, and yes, he too had been withdrawn these last months, but he loved her and he would try to be a better man. She believed it, but she knew too that he'd say anything to quieten her – and no, she would be heard or he could take his silent accusations and go. Yes, she'd failed appallingly. She was terribly, irredeemably guilty. She didn't need his eyes to tell her that. She felt it every second of every day. But she knew now too that the boy had not left them.

He crowbarred the water-butt away from the cottage wall, the feedpipe from the roof swinging like a limb, his shoulders straining. She watched from the kitchen window as he took a sledgehammer to the barrel, then a bottle of paraffin to make sure of the job and up it went, a cloud of black smoke from the wet wood hanging over the hillside like a pall.

And that was that. From now on, she stayed in her world and he in his, and they lived their grief alone. For a while, the novelty of his absence was a distraction, and she was glad of it. He stayed away from her at night too, preferring instead to sleep on the settee in the living room. For her part, she lay listening through the night as she always did but no sound came, just the sea-wind battering the walls again, playing the house with its whistles and skirls. Yet increasingly the dead came to her. Not Archie, but other children, their unblemished faces flowing towards her like a tide. Even in the full light of day, she'd feel their presence and know that if she closed her eyes they'd be there.

Not a word of this passed Celia's lips but Telfer knew her anguish. Lying at night in the living-room, he heard her bare feet on the bedroom floorboards above him and the creak of the bed betraying her wakefulness. He grieved for his son and for Celia now too, but whatever she believed, he did not hold her responsible for the boy's death. For Telfer, life had always been unpredictable. At sea, things happened that could not be legislated for. Likewise with the boy, no one was to blame, fate had intervened. Celia had always talked about the tube-train poster and how it had brought her to him – that chap who was his double and how, the next time she saw the poster on the train, someone had drawn a Hitler moustache on him and behind him a gentleman's privates emerged from the sea like the Loch Ness Monster. The poster was part of family lore now, even Grace knew about it, because it was the reason Celia and Telfer met, the reason for everything. But now when he tried to talk about Archie and fate or predestiny or whatever she wanted to call it, Celia accused him of wearing it as a mask to hide his hatred of her for what she had done, or rather what she had failed to do. No, the boy died because she wasn't paying attention and, if she couldn't forgive herself, how on earth could Telfer?

Tonight though, he'd had enough of his self-imposed exile on the living-room settee and, fearful of being turned away, he climbed the stairs to her, but her body welcomed him as he crept in beside her, and he fell into a deep sleep.

Celia lay there until his steady breathing became an invasion, then she wandered downstairs. There was no moon to light the corners of the room that night, no shadows to hide in, just a perfect stillness, and she stretched out on the living-room settee finding Telfer's shape indented into the cushions and closed her eyes.

She had no idea what time it was when she woke but she could feel Grace lying next to her, the girl's soft weight there. Celia lay still so as not to wake her but there it was again, that sound, quiet and insistent at first like tinnitus, then growing in volume – plaintive, pleading, keening – and somewhere inside it the drip, drip of water.

She reached for the oil lamp on the table next to the settee but it wasn't there – Telfer must've taken it up to bed with him – and now the keening was no longer distant, it was there in the room with them. Frightened that Grace would wake again, she wrapped her in a blanket to smother the sound, but her hands touched only air. Though the girl was present, absolutely present, there was no one there, and now what she thought was the girl's shape became his shape, his weight, his voice, unmistakably his voice, insensible at first, then his words coalescing into sentences – that he needed her, that he must have her. Wherever he was – here and yet not here – he was alone and frightened, and he needed his mother's comfort. But her arms could not find him.

From now on, the boy called out for her day and night, a siren sound that never once let up. He needed her physical touch, nothing else would do, and gradually the conviction took hold in her that, if he could not be here in this world with her, then she must be with him, wherever he was. But how? To go would mean leaving Grace behind. She'd be choosing one child's needs over the other and she could not do that, could she? No, if she was going to be with Archie then she had no choice but to take Grace with her.

One afternoon, the boy's pleading had grown into a breathless scream that shook the house and with it came an alignment of time and space she could no longer resist. The day had come. She knew it in her bones.

Grace was sitting at the kitchen table crayoning an expanse of blue sea when Celia slid a cottage pie out of the oven, its creamy cloud of potatoes browned just as the girl liked it. Telfer was out somewhere, they didn't know where, so Celia spooned out just two portions of the steaming deliciousness and sprinkled both plates with a salt of fine white dust – an entire bottle of sedatives to be shared between her and the girl.

Weren't they waiting for her father?

Let's eat it whilst it's hot.

The girl loaded her fork and brought it to her mouth, but it was scalding and the potato fell as it touched her lips.

Blow on it. Don't forget to blow.

Celia loaded the fork for her, imagining the mixture in the girl's throat, the action of swallowing, the drug travelling quickly through her little body to stop her heart. A split second, that was all it was, a snapshot of imagined time, then there it was in reality – the loaded fork, the girl's mouth closing around it and there was no turning back. In moments, the veil separating them from Archie would dissolve and the boy would be at peace.

Celia believed that this wasn't her choice to make, that she was powerless to resist the boy's insistence. But now, as the girl looked up and smiled, traces of the white potato clinging to her teeth and the corners of her lips, she had never seemed more alive and, before Grace could swallow, Celia reached over the table to stop her throat, and swept the child's mouth clean.

The house was growing dark when Telfer got home. In the kitchen, shards of broken china littered the floor and food spattered the cupboards and walls.

Outside in the garden he bellowed their names, but only the echo of his own voice came back.

Grace's crayoning sat on the kitchen table, a blue beach, the sand a mud brown. A scaly, black creature slithered over the land, hugging the contours of the coast. Not a creature, it was a train. What at first glance looked like scales were really windows.

Celia had been crayoning with her – the adult's hand alongside the child's drawings. Now, overlaying Grace's blue sea, a boy with yellow hair walked backwards into the water while beckoning a woman in a triangular dress to follow him. Telfer recognised it. It was the poster from the tube train – the beach, the train, the child, the woman – and he felt Grace's warm hand take his.

After her mother had swept her mouth, she'd run terrified from the house up onto the dunes and hidden herself there until she saw her father come home. Now, Grace turned the crayoning over for him and there was another drawing – this time in Celia's hand alone. The same yellow-haired boy but in black shadow, his mouth opened wide in a scream of anguish and horror and now, at last, Telfer understood what it was that Celia had been wrestling with these past months – her grief had been made flesh.

A track led away from the coast path and the boy ran on ahead disappearing around granite rocks that jutted out of the cliff face, Celia trying to keep pace with him.

That keening had finally stopped and, for once, there wasn't a breath of wind. When she reached the beach, the sky was clear and he was waiting for her in a patch of moonlight.

She sat with him as he played taking in his every movement and, for a while, time became elastic. There was no then or now, no life nor death, just the two of them in this moment. He occupied himself happily, barely glancing up for what might have been seconds or hours she could not tell, until finally his eyes held hers and she knew the moment had come.

She followed him down the beach, his bare feet not making a mark in the sand, until they reached the edge of the water and she froze. Was it doubt or just the ice-cold sea that made her hesitate? He was already up to his chest when he turned and beckoned to her, that yellow-haired boy gesturing to his mother, the poster come alive again – and she knew without doubt that this end was already present in the very beginning and she was powerless to resist it.

She waded on, the water licking around her waist and, for a second, she couldn't see the boy. Then there he was, swimming freely as he never could, his face appearing over the cresting waves, his eyes dancing. She shouted to him to wait for her and pushed further in until she was past the white horses, her clothes weighing her down.

Then hoping against hope that she might feel his hand in hers once again, she reached out – the water strangely silken and warm, phosphorescence on the surface of it like stars – and held him up, until at last he was in her arms and clinging to her, his blue eyes, his wide smile, his dimpled hands on her face until a wave submerged them and they fell deeper and deeper, the sea enfolding them. She held him close feeling what she thought she'd never feel again – his round, infant body, his breath, his kisses – and in the deep, dark water there was no separation between where he ended and she began, just one breathless soul falling.

But other hands held her now too, broader hands, strong arms pulling at her. She kicked and fought, the boy calling and calling, reaching out for her as he sank further and further into the dark. But no matter how she struggled, those arms, Telfer's arms, hauled her away until she broke the surface as the lights of a branch line train swept the beach and she was back on the London tube again where her glance at a poster had caught all that was to come.

She let Telfer hold her, feeling his warmth against the cold of the sea, her body shaping to his as her eyes scanned the waves wanting one more sighting. But there was nothing to see, just white horses cresting the blackness. And there standing in the water, the holding on inside of her let go and there was a leaving, a passing over. And she knew with all her being that everything there ever was will always be, and nothing and no one will ever die.

Author's Note

No one seems to know who wrote the music to 'Drink to me only with thine eyes' – it's referred to now as a traditional English folk tune, but the lyrics are from a poem by Ben Jonson called 'To Celia'. There are wonderful performances of it, not least by Johnny Cash, but for me the song brings to mind my late father's baritone still resonating down the decades.

The Blow In

Joanne Ella Parsons

There is so much to do today. The ash from the last residents' fire needs to be brushed away. Logs and kindling need to be placed in the old iron bucket that sits near the grate. The old-fashioned bed sheets – no duvets here – need turning down. I straighten the cluttered dresser in the kitchen. Move the teapot to one side and tuck the cosy neatly behind it. I take a glass from the shelf for the sprigs of *Calluna* – the last of this season's pink heather – and place it on the table. *Calluna vulgaris* for witches' brooms sweeping away the bad spirits, cleansing the cottage. The couple who will be staying here this weekend are late into their middle age. Watching them being greeted by the custodian, I could feel their gentle awkwardness – something in the way the air edged and crackled between their bodies, desperate to settle into its usual blanket of comfort and ease. Idly, I wonder if they are perhaps taking a trip away to recalibrate their lives and their relationship as their youngest leaves for university. Or could there be some tension in an otherwise good marriage that a few days away with fresh air and long walks can solve? They don't notice me – people rarely do – but I enjoy making up possibilities for their lives outside of our little cove.

Whatever they are here for, I wish them well.

I reach back down into my basket to leave an extra treat behind. A small bottle of brandy so they can have a tot by their fire tonight. I polish up two bulbous glasses with a faded tea towel, which I then fold and place by the sink.

Satisfied, I pick up my basket, give the old place a final sweeping check, casting my eyes over the downstairs, and head out into early afternoon light leaving the cottage unlocked – there is no need for caution and fear here.

The path down towards King's Cove is slightly slippy from the earlier mizzle which, despite the glimpses of sunshine trying to push through the clouds, is still hanging heavy in the air, misting the view across the sea. Never mind. There's no time to stop and look yet. My afternoon is full of chores and obligations. I can't check the Main House as it's been taken over by students from the university in Falmouth who come every year to lounge around, drink wine, and pretend to write. Bristling with annoyance at the mess I imagine them making, I sigh and move on, passing three young women going the other way with pens and paper in hands. Their laughter rises up and drifts across Bessy's Cove and out to sea.

'I can most assuredly tell you I booked it. You'll need to check again.'

I place my basket on the countertop and peep around the door frame. The custodian of the Cove is crossly checking the pages of the guest log looking for the details that match the irritated voice. I can see the white tufts poking out from under the custodian's woolly hat, which was hand-knitted by his wife who left this world some time ago.

'I don't see why I should have to suffer because you have made a stupid mistake. I really do not have time for this. This is your error and I suggest you start working very hard to fix it.'

The custodian, a big bear of a man, lifts his head from the log. There's menace in his calm. 'If you give me a moment, I'm sure we can sort this out. Please take a seat, while I make a call upstairs.' Brushing past me, the custodian has the measure of the man and so do I.

Following him out without even a cursory glance in my direction, the man lights up a cigarette with a gleaming silver lighter before pulling out his phone. The polished and waxed beard and moustache, the thick cable-knit sweater and old Barbour, the arrogance in how he holds himself all tell of a self-styled adventurer.

Anger makes his words spit down the phone.

'It's me. Absolute bloody incompetence. Are you sure you booked it?… Fine, it's hard to know when I'm surrounded by bloody idiots… Don't start. You know I need to get this done. It has to be on air by next week, especially as they blocked me from showing that place in Wales…'

I imagine him crossing lands and sea, diving in locations only accessible by a polluting boat while lecturing his viewers about the environment. Not respecting ownership or the voices of the past as he goes where he wants when he wants with no one to stop him.

'God damn it. Bloody place. Bloody signal.'

I leave him ranting at a dead phone line and turn around and head back to Coastguards, as the only cottage free this weekend is next to the couple who checked in earlier. I need to make sure it's ready for when the custodian brings him down. He won't like it, but I will do what I can.

The sea calls me as I emerge from under the canopy of trees that bow and stretch to reach each other across the cobbled path. I can taste its salt on my lips and feel its grains in my hair. Mordros – the sound of the sea – pulses in my heart and in my blood. The thump and the pull. It's all I've ever known. I look out over the old stone wall built by my grandfather's grandfather. It's getting dark now and the dusky ink of the sky blurs into the distant line of the horizon. It's impossible to tell where one ends and the other begins. The sea will have to wait. Later, I tell it. Later.

The couple are sitting on the old wooden bench outside their cottage enjoying the emerging stars in the sky and warming themselves with my brandy. There's little air between their bodies now and, what there is, is secure and calm. Their hands touch and they softly smile at each other, remembering who they are and what they mean to each other. Sometimes, it does not take very long at all for the Cove to work its magic.

The open-sided Land Rover grumbles as it chugs up the narrow track to the cottages. Abruptly stopping with a squeal, it spews the man out as the custodian opens the door on the other side. The custodian walks into the cottage, leaving the man to carry his suspiciously untarnished rucksack inside.

'I don't see why I have to pay for electricity on top… I'm used to rustic, but this is ridiculous… How am I meant to keep warm?' His bellyaching continues until he realises the toilet and shower are outside, allowing his annoyance to reach a crescendo of displeasure. The custodian waits for the grand finale, nods, and leaves.

Spying through the kitchen window at the back of the cottage, I see him making a performance of sniffing the now musty stale air, before pushing aside the delicate white blooms of sea campion I left out for him so he can roll out an old map of the coastline.

I leave him to it and head down to the sea.

The next morning starts bright and light. There is a slight breeze, but it will be one of the last few good days before the winter sets in. I walk down to the cove; the steps are steep and uneven, but I don't stumble. I lay my jacket on a rock, slip off my shoes and the rest of my clothes. I refuse to look at the etching on my skin – scars from a past trauma that still haunts, and instead turn my eyes to the skyline. The water is quiet today. My feet sink into the tiny pebbles as I walk into the water. I breathe through the chill of the sea, slowly circling my limbs in breaststroke, letting my breathing and my mind calm. I swim until I feel blueness bloom in my lips and prickles of cold tingle down my limbs, but I am still reluctant to turn back, to return to my daily chores, to folding the sheets, to overseeing the guests, to lighting fires, and to leaving my welcome gifts. Later, I will have to do my rounds but, for now, this moment and the safety of Bessy's Cove belongs to me, and it has never let me down. This collection of coves has been my home for longer than I care to remember and, if you treat them well, your kindness will be returned threefold. Time has taught me that.

He is holding court. Trapped, the couple next door are unable to open up an opportunity for escape. I move closer. He is pontificating and lecturing them on the history of Prussia Cove, practising his lines so that he can record them later.

'Of course, it is well known that John Carter was smuggling goods in and out of Bessy's Cove back in the late 18th century. They say he was a Methodist and renowned for his honesty. But that was hardly likely. Those were hard days and they were hard men. Violent sorts. He was something of a local celebrity in his time. One of the collection of coves that make up Prussia Cove, King's Cove is named after him, John Carter, the King of Prussia. What a joke! A labouring class hero, if you will…'

He was not hard. He was kind. He only took what belonged to him or what he needed. Had the man done his research he would have found the oft-repeated story of how excise officers had intercepted one of John's deliveries from France. He stole his goods back from the Custom House stores but took not a single item that was not his. Any fool knows that, and those that don't can easily find out. The sea thuds its displeasure.

'But of course a famous man must have his women. And by God John Carter did! The worst of them being Bessy, a local landlady who sold his plundered alcohol in her bar and sold herself on the side too no doubt. A wanton woman! That's what they'd have called her in those days. Well, the politer folk would have. But the men who worked on the boats and in the fields would have called her something much riper I don't doubt! She was definitely known for her sluttish and slovenly ways! But aren't all women guilty of something?'

The couple shift uneasily as the man winks, and my anger rises with the wind.

'They say there's a tunnel between one of the coves leading to one of the houses. It has long been sealed but if anyone can locate it, then I'm your man. Correct?! I've uncovered plenty of surprising things before. You should watch my show – you could learn more than a thing or too.'

Pleased with himself, he slams the door behind him as he goes into his cottage to gather his camera and tripod.

The sea crashes against the rocks and I feel my body tighten as I urge him to not raise the bones of the dead, but the words never leave my mouth.

I cannot settle all day. I try to stomp out my discomfort across the coastal path to Praa Sands, but the steep drops make me uneasy and I have to turn back. The clumps of *Calluna* are fading fast and there is barely a whisper of its scent in the air. Soon the stiff branches of winter will be wrapped around us and summer will feel a long time away.

Wherever I roam, the cove circles me back to the man. I cannot turn without stumbling across him reciting his lines into a camera or recording notes on his phone. I am forced to watch him plotting his version of John Carter's truth and poking at the secrets Bessy took pains to hide. He runs his hand along the deep grooves carved into the rocks from the carts used to haul the loot from sea to cave and back again. They are smooth and polished from past industry.

The smell of burning lures me up the path again. The students are having a fire at King's Cove and telling stories, and it seems that the man is not the only one who has heard tales of John Carter and Bessy. I catch snatches of their imaginations as they tell tales of Bessy's heroics and John Carter's mischief. They see fun and camaraderie and adventure. They imagine the outline of ghostly ships laden with precious cargo that don't come here any more. They mash up past and present and play with new futures. There's hope in the young. I leave them to their games.

Nightfall almost saves me, but one final pull brings me to Coastguards. The man stands behind the small row of cottages wrapped up in scarves and jumpers to protect against the whip and sting of the night air. The noise of his anger pushing the quiet away. He should be careful. He does not understand the rules here.

He is on his phone again, rolling his eyes at the muffled voice pleading with him from some other place. A place that protects men like him.

'I don't understand why you have to be like this. You always make things into a problem. I don't know why I ever bothered with you. You're never happy. You're lucky I stayed around…'

My scars itch and burn as I feel the tension that must be held in the woman's body at the end of the line. I know she is crying.

'It's bad enough being stuck here trying to find this bloody passageway in this godawful place without having to deal with you as well. I'm damn sure it's at Bessy's Cove… It must be. I will not be leaving until I've found it. So you can stop bitching at me and let me do what I need to do.'

I pace my breathing like I've entered the sea. I know what will happen now. The cove does too. We beat and we rise and we wail. Our fury stiffens the spikes of the maritime pines, sharpens the rocks hiding in the sea, coats the paths with our salty spit. And we have time to wait.

'I don't know why you have to be such a cow about it. I don't give a damn what you think...' Venom crawls out of his mouth. The smooth face he shows to his public twists and cracks. Eyes hard. Disgust scrawled in the curve of his mouth. But we have always seen him for who he is.

Angrily he terminates the call. He throws his cigarette on the ground, crushing the glowing butt underfoot before stomping back into the house. Shoulders raised like the hackles of a beast. The curtains are drawn but I can see his shadow glowering behind them. Tension crackles, and I hear the sea's curses smashing into the land.

I head to my place of safety. Doubling back to the entrance to Bessy's Cove, each step takes me closer to a greater ominous certainty. Someone's torch casts an eerie light over the sea, making the pitch black of the world and the night sky more claustrophobic. I trace my finger over the raised patterns that crisscross over my skin, snaking their way up my arms and across my body. My scars burn in a way that never happened when they were new. Then, I was too numb to feel anything when the Revenue men's gunfire set our boat alight and I saw the flames dance and drown in the sea.

Days later, I leave the couple's cottage after preparing it for the new guests. This time, a young couple and their dogs will be joining us. Here to walk and fall in love all over again.

'Hello! I'm so sorry to bother you but I was wondering if you could help me?' Startled, I stare at the unexpected visitor approaching the custodian, who has just delivered fresh bundles of wood for the cottages' fires. 'It's just that my husband came here for work you see – he makes films – and I haven't heard from him and he's supposed to be up the other end of the country by now. It's not unusual for him to just go but I had this feeling. It's silly really, but you know when you get a feeling?'

The custodian nods. The visitor's tense and I notice that her nose has been broken at some point. She is still achingly beautiful, but so thin and so sad.

He shows her into the cottage and tells her she is welcome to look around and, if she needs him, she can find him in his office at the top of the hill. The door closes and I move to the back of the cottage to watch her entering the kitchen where the old map has been kept open with teacups and the sugar pot. She spots his camera on the table beside the wilting sea campion – witches' thimbles, Devil's hatties, dead men's bells – call it what you will. I hang back, leaving her to her discoveries.

She picks up the camera, and presses play. Her eyes follow those of her husband's as he heads down the treacherous steps to Bessy's Cove, certain he is on the trail of something significant. He turns suddenly and she holds her breath as the camera shakes in fear while the waves crash. She lifts her hand to her mouth, and I know she can smell the salty air and panic as if she was there. The camera drops and watches her husband scramble up the rocks – his terror making him reckless and desperate – before he is taken by the sea. She rewinds the film but, as she watches for a second time, a smudge catches her eye, haunting the frame. Pausing, she zooms in and sees the blurred edges of a woman in the distance waiting for the sea to finish its task.

The visitor rushes out, breath shallow, and pulled by an invisible force. Gasping the air fresh from the sea, her breathing calms. I am close enough to hold her, but she cannot see me.

I watch her walk back inside the house, stooping her head slightly to avoid the low beam. She sits on the window seat in the living room and deletes the film.

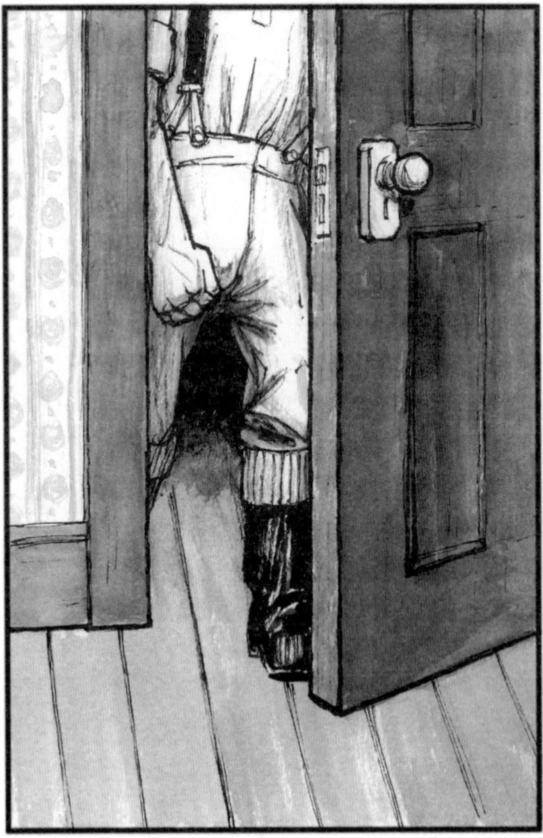

Till Death Do Us Part

Tony Cowell

Falmouth, November 1945

Night was falling with visible speed, like a black sea creeping over the earth. Nelly stared out of the bedroom window at the moon casting shadows over the gravestones, wishing she had never agreed to move to a house overlooking a cemetery.

Nelly was plagued by a recurring nightmare:

The sinking ship lurched as its bow dipped beneath the waves. The stern remained above the water for a few seconds, before plunging downwards at great speed. The icy water chilled her body as it dragged her down beneath the surface. Reaching into the darkness, she desperately searched for his hand, but found only oily seaweed threaded between her fingers. Gasping for air, she climbed onto the wreckage of the vessel, clinging to the debris with her remaining strength, Nelly screamed into the soulless night. Once again, she reached down into the sea which had begun to burn, and the flames were coming closer. Snatching her arm from the water, she stared in horror at the bloodied stump where her hand had once been. Then nothing… only the roar of the raging ocean as it slowly began to swallow her.

Dawn was breaking as Nelly locked the bathroom door behind her. Her heart was racing, pounding high in her chest. She stared at Jacob's cut-throat razor. A beam of watery light swept the room as she rubbed her fingers down the spine of the blade. She felt the cool surface of the pearlescent handle and sensed the hairs on her neck rise as she recalled a moment from the past. Glancing at her reflection in the mirror, she wondered what it would feel like to die.

She decided not to tell Jacob about the nightmares, he wouldn't understand.

In the kitchen, Nelly made breakfast as Jacob sat quietly at the table reading the paper. She made him a pot of tea and a sandwich to take to work, which she placed in front of him, wrapped in a brown paper bag. Nelly sat down, careful not to disturb him, and cradled her cup between her palms. She stared over at her husband.

'Do you know when you'll be home?' she asked. Jacob sighed and pulled his fob watch from his jacket, ignoring her question. As Nelly took her cup to the sink, the back door slammed, shaking the thin walls. She looked down at the abandoned sandwich and slowly picked it up, placing it under a glass bowl in the pantry. Perhaps he will eat it when he returns from the Docks, she thought.

Later that afternoon Doctor Webster arrived. The light was fading fast as Nelly brought him coffee and sat to face him after straightening the cushions on the chairs. It was how Jacob liked the sitting room to look, ordered and smart. Nelly always looked forward to the GP's visits; he was the only man that made her feel safe. He tapped his pipe on the ashtray before refilling it and lighting it with a match. Nelly smoothed her pleated skirt and began to tell him about the nightmares, and then her fears about Jacob.

'Sometimes, I think I am losing my mind,' she told him.

Doctor Webster looked down at his hands, as puffs of smoke hung in the air like an early morning fog.

'You are in a constant state of worry, Nelly, that's all – the war has made us all this way. We often begin to imagine situations that are not always real. So many of us are still struggling to get our lives back, which is why I am going to give you something to help you sleep.'

Out of the corner of her eye Nelly caught a sudden movement by the door. The cat jumped up and settled on her lap, his pale yellow eyes staring up at her knowingly, as if conveying a warning. Bozley had arrived at the house the night war was declared and had never left her side.

Dr Webster smiled at the cat and took it as a sign to leave. He placed the box of pills he had prescribed on the table and bid Nelly goodbye.

That night, as Nelly climbed the stairs, she paused to stare at a photograph. Outside, the wind was gathering pace, thin branches scraped the windows. The picture was taken on her wedding day in the chapel at Helston. It wasn't the happy memory it should have been. Her eyes travelled the length of Jacob's body and settled on his hand gripping her forearm. She could still feel his pinching fingers digging into her skin through her thin dress. She had dared to walk ahead of him for a brief moment and he'd pulled her back. Her misery was captured on film, an eternal reminder of the day she had trapped herself at Jacob's hand. Once again, the wind howled making the house groan as it braced against the violent gusts.

As she lay in bed, listening to the trees straining against the fierce wind, she thought the sound akin to a caged animal: a beast begging to be released, its angry cries of despair becoming a constant feral roar. The grandfather clock struck midnight, and the wooden stairs began to creak. Nelly held her breath, begging for sleep, but it felt as if the air had been sucked out of the room. The wind continued to whip up a frenzy of dark whispers that stealthily crept into each corner of the house.

Suddenly, she felt Jacob's cold hand on her shoulder and her whole body froze as if turned to ice. She remained as still as she could, hoping he would tire of torturing her. There was a short pause before she heard his voice – it was low and measured and sounded hollow in the cold, damp room. It made her heart thump in terror. It always did.

'Do you ever wish you could change the past, Nell?'

Nelly turned her head towards him, trying to stop herself from trembling, but it was futile. She could make out his angular features in the moonlight; his profile repulsed her and she wished him away, shutting her eyes tightly. She felt the tears escape, tracking down her cheeks as she struggled to compose herself.

'You can't change time. The past is the past, Jacob. We can't alter that. Now the war is over, the future is surely our only protector. We both need to move on.'

Jacob's voice became more insistent, as she met his grey gaze. 'But what if we could go back and conceive a different plan. It is all I ever think of, Nell, apart from you.' He continued to stare at her – and his eyes grew dark and watery, and he began to laugh, as if mocking her. 'What is it you are so afraid of, Nell… is it me?'

Nelly's breathing became agitated. She turned away from him

unable to respond to his question as fear gripped her.

'Please, let me rest, Jacob. This can wait till the morning. Every time you talk about the past, it makes me realise how the war changed us all. We are no longer the same.'

When eventually sleep came, her dreams took over but this time they were different. She was travelling through a long dark tunnel. At first, it felt threatening and devoid of hope, as if her world was suddenly tilting on its axis. As she drifted deeper into the night, she failed to hear the heavy breathing close to her ear, and the persistent rapping at the kitchen door.

The following morning Nelly woke at dawn. Bozley began to purr loudly, nudging her face with his bony head. She gently stroked his ears and the purring stopped abruptly. She could hear Jacob's footsteps in the kitchen.

Glancing at the bedside table she noticed his fob watch was missing. In the bathroom mirror, her face appeared softer; it was the first night she had slept without reliving her nightmare. Perhaps Dr Webster had been right after all; the pills were easing her worry. In her heart, she instinctively knew her life had to change. She needed to believe she had a future – instead of being haunted by her past.

Downstairs, she gazed out of the kitchen window towards the cemetery and noticed the wind had receded. The fir trees were virtually static, but the giant oak swayed gently, as if its branches were waving to her. She began to brew tea, and placed two cups on the table, along with a slice of toast from the last of her weekly loaf.

Out of the corner of her eye, she saw Jacob leaning against the kitchen door. She immediately felt the bile rise from her stomach and was overwhelmed by a terrifying sickness. She began to back away until she had nowhere else to go, before gripping the countertop so hard, her knuckles turned white. Her body stiffened as she faced him. There was a deadness in the silence between them.

Jacob stamped his boots on the mat. He was smirking and rubbing the stubble on his chin. He moved to the crockery on the draining board and inspected it, turning each piece over in his hand. He fixed her with a look of disgust as he swept the cups back into the dirty water in the sink, sending splashes over the floor she'd just scrubbed. His voice was dark and menacing.

'I sense a change in you, Nell, and you look… somehow different. I want you to know I am still here. I must keep you near, but I think you've always known that.'

His voice began to sound muffled and distant. Nelly hesitated, not wanting to answer. She felt a need for justice, and an end to all the drama of the past. She couldn't live in this torment for another moment. She knew it was time. Bozley looked up from his food and stared blankly at the kitchen door, his fur ruffling slightly as if someone was stroking him. Nelly took her coat from the hook. As she hurried out of the front door, the gulls began circling overhead, crying into the air. A pale, thin sunlight lit her face as she walked briskly towards the cemetery gates. Marching up the steep slope, her breathing became heavy until she reached the mound where the fresher graves had been dug. Glancing back at the house, she hesitated, imagining a face watching her from the kitchen window. She turned away, dismissing the idea that she could hear him screaming her name. A single white cloud momentarily hid the sun, and a gentle breeze kissed her skin.

Nelly knelt beside Jacob's grave and stared up at the grey

marble with absent fascination. She began to nervously fiddle with the wilted lilies in the vase, ripping them out and throwing them across the grave. She looked up at the sky, as if in search of inspiration. Inhaling deeply, she began to whisper.

'There was a time when you convinced me you were still here, but now I know you are not. Today is the day I have to be strong, and finally be free of you. There is nothing left of you in this world, so I want you gone. I begged you not to step foot on that ship, and by doing so you set your own course. I live each day as if I am locked in a dark, forbidden world with no escape. Do you recall when we first took our vows, we promised to love till death do us part? Well, now we have, and our life together is over, and for that I am grateful. I yearn to live the rest of my life in peace, without you. Now, at last, I realise just how happy that could make me.'

In the silence that followed, Nelly slowly stood, smiling as she gazed down at Jacob's grave. The seabirds hovered overhead, and she felt her sadness lift, yielding to a renewed lightness in her step as she walked back to the house.

A heavy rain was falling, and the trees were already awash with shadow as Doctor Webster knocked at the door. Nelly showed him to his usual chair by the fire and set the tea tray down on the table, before finally summoning the strength to tell him what he probably already knew about Jacob, and her life with him.

'I remember him sitting in that same chair, and he looked me straight in the eye. "I'm going to war," he said. It was 1.30 in the morning when he slipped out of the house, on his secret mission. Back then, I wished to God he had never set foot on that wretched ship. He wasn't even a navy man; he was a merchant seaman – yet he was determined to go and fight. To do his bit. When they eventually found him, they wouldn't let me see his body, it was too burnt. Unrecognisable they said. It was in that moment that I realised something. I was finally free of him. I didn't need to see his dead body. I never wanted to see him again. But yet I do. I see him every day.'

Dr Webster shifted uneasily in his chair, as Nelly refilled his teacup before continuing.

'Do you know why I married Jacob? Because I don't. I think I was so terrified of him. He had a temper, and could be very difficult, and I don't think I ever loved him. I used to believe that one day I'd eat my last meal with him in this house and then run, run as far away from him as I could. I never did of course. I let him control me.' Nelly felt the tears come, and she quickly stifled a sob. 'He was never kind to me, ever. He never wanted to make me happy. I was just a wife. Someone who was willing to keep the peace. The irony is, the dead are so much freer than the living, and in a way I resent that. The dead always want to tell their own story so that they can selfishly rest in peace. That's why I often question what death really has to say about the human condition.'

The grey light was waning fast, and the house was already veiled in a deepening dusk. Doctor Webster crossed his legs and cleared his throat. He lit his pipe then dropped the match into the ashtray and watched it burn. Nelly realised the cushions weren't straight on the armchairs. Her muscles twinged with a longing to fix them, but she resisted.

'Nelly, the shadow of war still hangs over us all. What I have come to understand is that pathological grief is when a bereaved person finds it impossible to move on. They say grief is simply love with nowhere to go. But love is not always what the mind imagines, but what the heart feels. I believe you may be ready to move on.'

He smiled at her and slowly reached over and touched her cheek, holding his hand there a moment longer than he should. She nodded but her face remained impassive. She could feel the warmth of his stare and realised it was the first time she had seen him smile.

She took his hand and gently squeezed it. In that moment, she suddenly began to understand the depth of love that had been missing from her life and, above all, kindness. She could hardly recall what kindness was supposed to feel like. She fetched his fedora and overcoat as he stood by the door facing her. 'I wondered if next week, Dr Webster, you might like to stay for supper. Nothing fancy, but it would be… nice, perhaps.' She looked up at him hopefully as a blush spread across her pale skin.

'I'd like that, Nelly, thank you,' he replied. He tipped his hat and smiled warmly at her. 'I'd like that very much. And Nelly, please call me William.'

After he left, she locked the back door, fed Bozley his kibble, and went to bed. This time there were no dreams or nightmares. At precisely 1.30 a.m., the wind began to howl through the trees in the cemetery and a light came on in the kitchen. As Nelly slept, Bozley jumped down from the bed and began to meow, scratching at the bedroom door. He padded down the stairs towards the kitchen.

The next morning Nelly listened to Prime Minister Clement Attlee's speech on the wireless as she fed Bozley. Standing at the kitchen window she thought about Dr Webster and smiled. William. As she looked towards the cemetery, she felt a sense of calm engulf her body. She turned to see two teacups on the draining board and was suddenly overcome with nausea. She held her breath for a moment, then slowly placed Jacob's cup in the kitchen cabinet, pushing it to the back of the shelf, gently shutting it away. Forever. At the same moment, Bozley raised his head from his bowl, staring at the kitchen door as it slowly began to open.

A grey mist began to form into a dark, familiar shape.

Author's Note

In March 1942, more than 600 men left Falmouth in a flotilla of three destroyers and 16 smaller boats, including HMS *Campbeltown*, which was packed with explosives. The ship rammed into the gates of the docks in St Nazaire, France. Dozens of British servicemen and merchant seamen were killed in the raid. Operation Chariot was one of the most daring and courageous missions of WWII.

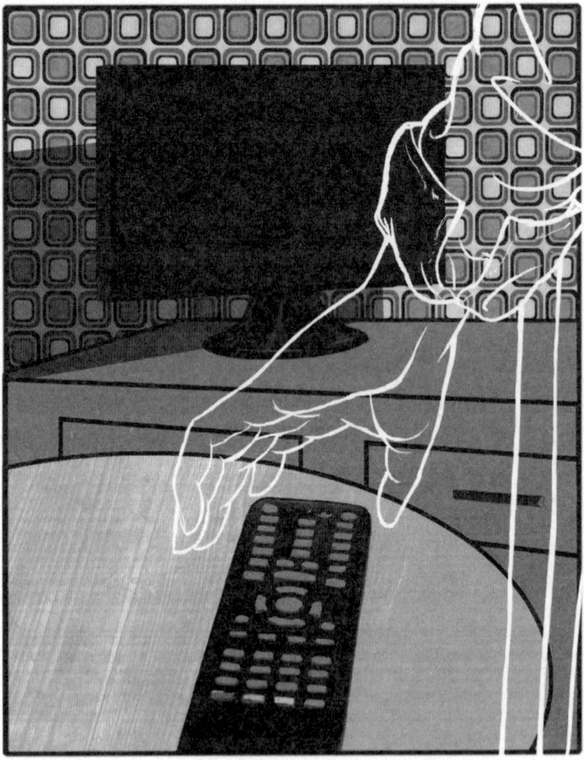

The Trouble with Being Dead

Emily Barr

The trouble with being dead is that you can't talk to anyone. Actually, that's not true: I talk to you all the time. You just don't hear me. Now, for example. You are going to be late to work and I am yelling into your ear. 'Lily! Lily! Lilylilylilylilylily!'

Your face is smooshed into a cushion, and you are dribbling a bit. I pull back and look at you and I'm torn. You look so pretty when you sleep, even when you're drooling. You're nearly thirty and you're still beautiful, though you don't know it. My favourite thing about you is the fact that you breathe. I sit on your bed and watch you, every single night. That's how I know that you didn't sleep last night, that your alarm was set for seven but that you gave up just before five, came downstairs, made a coffee, and picked up the remote control.

Coffee and a remote control. Two things you take for granted. Two things I would kill for.

You need to wake up. I switch into my own cottage and look around. I've been hoarding the things in here for a long time, and this might be time to use one. I click back to yours and think about it.

You won't hear me unless I do something drastic. Really I want you to stay on the sofa asleep in front of our favourite programme (*Married at First Sight Australia*, duh). It's nearly too late for you to make it to work on time anyway. You need to wash and blow dry that hair if you're going to make any kind of positive impression, and your car key has slipped off the shelf where you leave it and is in your shoe, so we're going to have to spend ten minutes looking for that too. We haven't got ten minutes.

If I leave you, you'll wake at about ten o'clock and realise what you've done and cry and curl up in despair and feel... No, let's not do that. When you feel things strongly, I feel them too and I haven't got the strength for that.

I stare for a moment at the remote control. If I had control of that I'd turn the volume up on Domenica and Jack until they woke you. You have no idea how lucky you are, Lily. You have TV, and also cars have been invented and, not only are you allowed to drive, but you actually have your own car and it's bright red (good choice). The idea of having to marry a stranger is so alien that you watch people doing it on telly, for entertainment. You are allowed to have all the boyfriends you like, not that you get any further than swiping a bit on Tinder and ignoring the messages that come in. If you preferred girls, it would be completely fine. You don't, though. The guy you like is not from Tinder. He's called Sam French and you see him in real life. I'm hoping you'll bring him home with you one day, but I'm not sure he knows you exist.

You learned to read when you were a tiny child and now you have hundreds of books. You live in a very different Cornwall from the one I knew. All of that would have been miraculous to me. It *is* miraculous.

Lilylilylilylily. I cup my hands around your ear and yell it with everything I've got. It's a strange thing, your name. The same syllable again and again and again. Things lose all meaning after a while. Anyway, I keep going. *Lily*.

It's early days – you've only been in my house for two months – and that's frustrating. It takes me years to get through to people and then when I do they scream and move out saying it's haunted. One day I'm going to push beyond the bit where they become aware that I'm here. One day I'm going to do the next part: I'm going to make friends. And you, Lily, are the best target so far. You need a friend almost as much as I do.

I pop into my own version of the house and go to the scullery for my mixing bowl.

Our cottage is down a track not far from St Austell, which in my day was a little village of no consequence at all. I've pieced it together over the years from the people who've come and gone. Long after my time, the tin mining started up and brought in money. St Austell had the greatest tin mine in the world, and even from here I was proud of us. Then they built the main road to London and after that we got china clay pits and riches beyond anything we'd have imagined. My little village was properly on the map! Then of course things went downhill, though I'd like to visit that Eden Project. And the brewery. The train station.

As I said, you've lived here two months, Lily, whereas I've been around for, what, three hundred and eighty years, give or take? You lose track, but it's 2022 and I was born in 1636, and died in 1653 so I guess I'm 386 years old, seventeen of them alive. And you know what? I still look younger than you do. Lol. I was born, lived a life that was both joyous and fucking awful, and died in this cottage, and I've not been beyond the garden gate ever since. I long to get out there and run down to West Polmear to look at the ocean. Go and see what these clay pits were all about. Drive a car, catch a train, go on the internet. Eat food. Breathe air. Make coffee and pick up the remote control. All those things you do. I want them.

Anyway. We need to get you to work, my love, don't we, for your first day at County Hall? Past St Austell and all the way to Truro, which would have taken a long time in my day but when you put it into your phone map it said it'll take thirty-one minutes! Less than one *Selling Sunset*.

I decide to fetch the mixing bowl.

I live in two cottages: the one I died in, and the one that's changed over the years. They're superimposed on each other. I move between the two of them, flicking between my world and yours just by choosing to do it. I have been saving my best old bowl for an emergency, and I think this might be it. I pick it up and head into my parlour. I stand on the spot where you are currently asleep, hold the bowl over my head, and lob it down onto the tiles. It smashes into gazillions of pieces, and the sound is so loud it makes me gasp and laugh. I shift into your world and stare at you.

You stir. I am beginning to get through. I knew it.

You were so determined to be organised this morning, Lily. You've made a packed lunch and put your 'pantsuit' out ready. It's all gone tits up, my love, because you self-sabotaged (that's from the motivational YouTube video we watched when you got the job). I watched you not-sleeping all night long.

It's not fair that you don't know I exist. I can pour out my troubles to you and the pinnacle of what I might get in return is a vague sense of the house, settling. Though you're not overburdened with friends, are you? You have the whole living world out there, at your feet, and you stay home with me. It was your twenty-ninth birthday last week and you got four cards. Four! In my day, we didn't have the tradition of folding up bits of card and giving them to someone to mark special occasions. I wish we had – I'd have loved it, and I'd have had a hell of a lot more than four, I can tell you. I was popular. I was the most popular girl in the village, and that was my downfall. *You* got four cards, and one of them was from the life insurance company. Actually, you got five, but you couldn't see the best one. Took me ages, that did.

At five, you made a coffee while I sat on the counter and watched. I wish I knew what coffee tasted like. I can only just smell it (I had to practise hard to get there), but it's a good smell all right. You drink five cups on some days, if you haven't slept. You put oat milk in it. In my day, milk came from the cow but, since we watched that thing, I've been totally on board with your oat milk. Can't work out though why it costs less to raise a cow, get it pregnant, take its baby away and steal that baby's milk, than it does to grow some oats and squeeze them. You live in a strange world, Lily.

A strange and brilliant world. You have everything out there, at your fingertips and you don't do a thing with it. No one's gonna marry you off. Quite the opposite. You don't have to have ten babies in the hope that a couple of them make it through childhood to run the farm. You can be weird without being called a witch. You can do anything, go anywhere. And here's what you do:

nothing.

I crouch down and pick up the biggest remnants of mixing bowl. I throw them on the floor again, all at once. It does the job. You give a little jolt and open your eyes. Look around, confused. A tiny smile at the *Married at First Sight* dinner party before you remember. You grab your phone and stare at it. Two minutes to eight. Seventeen minutes until you need to leave if you're going to park and get to your desk by nine. You're welcome.

'Shit!' You shout it out loud. I like that: it means you're talking to me even if you don't know it.

'Shit!' I shout back. When you do speak, you say *shit* a lot. That's why I do, too. I grin at you and watch you working out what you have to do. No time to wash that hair. You scrape it into a ponytail which is just about OK. Spray a fuckton of deodorant. Put on some make-up (Lily: red lipstick is never going to suit you however much you want it as armour. It'd be great on me, but there we go). You ordered a dark blue pantsuit for work after looking at pictures of Hillary Clinton, but you don't carry it off like she did (don't get me started on the people voting for that man instead of her: when you've come up against it once you see it everywhere). It actually looks OK on you though, and then you're putting on your work shoes – sadly the car key is in a trainer – and you're grabbing your bag and at exactly quarter past eight the hunt for the key begins. Even though I yell 'In the shoe!' one million times over you don't check it for nine minutes. Then you find it and run. Your packed lunch remains on the side in the kitchen, Lily. I hope there's somewhere to get food out there at County Hall or you'll be extra tired and cranky this afternoon. I hope you can get a nice coffee with oat milk. I don't like you being away from me. I am going to worry non-stop.

I get into the car with you, just for fun. I sit in the passenger seat and pretend to click my seatbelt into place when you do yours. I even make a clicky noise with my mouth. You start the engine. I say *Brrrmmm brrrmmm*. God I'd love to drive.

Put the radio on!

You don't. It's because you want to psych yourself up as you go. Fine – I won't be here for long anyway. We set off bumping down the track, a bit too fast for the suspension. I wish I could go to County Hall with you. I can't even imagine what it's like up Truro these days. I used to know it as a port, safe from pirates and all that because it was up the river. Rich, with all the riches from the mining even before the St Austell mines existed. The most magical market days. I'd love to see it in your world: I've seen no more than the odd glimpse on the local news and to be honest it wasn't the city of wonder and awe that I'd been imagining, but maybe that's just because when I see it it's on news reports about shoplifting or shit weather.

We're approaching the end of the track.

'Bye my darling!' I shout. 'You can do it! I love you!'

Then you drive through the gate, and I'm ejected from the car. I land on my arse on the stones and sit there for a bit, waving to you. I pick myself up, shake out my skirts, and set off back home to wait.

It's not the same on my own, that's for sure. I stare at the telly but nothing I do makes it switch on. I read the spines of your books, again. I learned to read in about 1900 when there was a little boy here being taught his letters by his mother, but I can't read the pages because they're all closed. Sometimes I try to imagine the stories that might live inside them. *The Handmaid's Tale* – I know that one because I watched it with the last people who lived here.

I'd love to read it. *The House in the Olive Grove*: that sounds nice. *Under a Cornish Sky*. Yes please. The only book in my cottage is the Bible, and to be honest I'm over it. Fat lot of good it ever did me.

When you're here, Lily, I think about you. When you're not, I have to think about me. I wasn't like you in life. As I said, I was full of it. I talked, I sang, I danced. I was friends with everyone. I didn't see why I, Maggie Cock (it was a common name, all right?), couldn't do what my four brothers did. I wanted to learn everything. To see everything. I was curious. I'd have gone far, like Hillary, if I was born now, but not so much back then.

I was mouthy, and I loved a girl. We kept it quiet, but you can't keep things properly quiet in a place like this.

Long story short, there were menfolk in the village who had no truck with me. They wanted to shut me up. I was supposed to get married, and it was pretty much married at first sight which, yes, is why that show is my favourite. It helps me work through my own past trauma, I guess. I didn't want to marry Petroc Harris for obvious reasons, so I said no. If I'd been on *Married at First Sight* I'd have been one of the awkward women who doesn't take the bullshit. Petroc Harris took his hurty ego and went and told everyone I was a witch. Everyone, of course, believed him. Calling mouthy women witches was all the rage, even here in Cornwall, and then they found out about me and Grace. Everyone turned on me. All my friends, Lily. Even my own brothers switched sides. It was honestly just like it is these days. A pile-on. I was cancelled. Same human nature, different tech.

I was ready to defend myself at the trial. My parents said no: they said I was bringing shame on the family, that I actually was possessed by the devil and that I was a witch and all the other things people say (neither of them could look me in the eye as they knew it was bullshit) and they tried to exorcise the devil out of me and, long story short, they overdid it and I died. Right here, in this room.

Oh Lily! Come home!

I check the time: five past eleven. Hours and hours to go, and I seem to be crying. Maggie! Stop it! I don't cry.

In my world, I go for a walk round the garden. I tend to my flowers. I sweep up all the bits of mixing bowl. In yours, I mime flicking the kettle on and pretend to make a coffee.

By the time you get home, I have a plan. I've gathered all my pans and piled them next to me at the place where the stairs go round the corner. I'm ready. I hear the car door slamming and prep myself. There's your key in the lock. I catch your misery coming through the door before you do.

You need a friend. I need a friend. Let's do this.

As you stand just inside the door kicking your shoes off, I get to work. I throw a pan at you, and another and another and another. Every one of them hits you in the head because I do have a great aim. I've practised, over the years. I'm like Robin Hood in that movie, but with pans instead of arrows. I'm sorry to do this, because I love you, but I have to keep trying.

The last pan is my old milk pan. Small but powerful. It gets you on the forehead and…

And…
And…
And…
you rub your head.

You rub your fucking head. You do it exactly where the pan hit you.

You look up, right at me. For a second, it's as if you see me.

'Lily!' I shout it as loud as I can. 'Lily! It's OK! I love you!'

Just for a moment, our eyes meet.

You close your eyes. Open them again. Shake your head. I follow you into the bathroom and watch while you do a really long wee, wash your hands (not thoroughly enough! Some of us have seen a real plague), and take two paracetamol. I stand next to you, watching the whole time.

'Lily.' I whisper it into your ear. 'Lilylilylilylilylily.'

You look at me. Frown slightly. Shake your head again. You keep shaking your head because you're denying it to yourself. And that means that there's something that needs denying, and that means we're getting there. We are, at last, starting to connect. This is the bit where I really hope you won't move out of the house and tell everyone it's haunted like those guys did last time. I don't think you will. Something happened to make you move to a cottage down a bumpy track on your own and whatever it was (you've never spoken about it out loud) I don't think me talking to you is going to change it. Whatever it was that brought you here is stronger than me spooking you.

'No,' you whisper. You hit yourself on the side of the head.

'YES!' I shout.

I have to be patient. This is a breakthrough but it's gonna take time.

I work on you for ages. I devote myself to you, more than ever. I talk into your ear. I tell you I'm your friend. I whisper my life story to you while you sleep. I tell you all about me and Grace because even after hundreds of years I love talking about her. I think a few weeks pass. We're nearly at the final commitment ceremonies on *Married at First Sight Australia*, and you're almost as invested as I am. You go to work at your new job five days a week, and you hate it, sadly, like the last one. I had hoped it would be the making of you, but no such luck. Once a week you speak to your mum on the phone. Always on a Sunday, always at six. I lean right in, trying to hear exactly what she's saying.

'Yeah, it's good,' you say. 'It's going well.' You wipe your eyes with the back of your hand as you say it. Sometimes you hold the phone away from your ear so you can cry, then pull it back and say, 'No: I'm fine. Honestly. Just got a bit of a cold.'

I have no idea what your mother is like but I think that, if I were you, I'd tell her to fuck off. You ask her, sometimes, if she's going to come and visit and, even though I can't really hear her, it's easy enough for me to work out that she's saying no. She's making excuses. She's saying Cornwall is too far away, that it would be easier for *you* to go to *her*. Erm – hello? If Cornwall's too far away for her to visit you, then isn't wherever she lives also too far away for you to visit her? I wish you'd say that, but you never do. I would.

Though also I'd get on a train and go all over the place. I'd get right out of here.

Oh Lily. Life is wasted on you. It's passing you by.

And then you speak to me.

It happens after the next series of *Married at First Sight* has finished. We're watching an old season of *Below Deck Sailing Yacht* instead. I'm next to you, trying to hold your hand, talking to you. I like *Below Deck* but it's not my favourite and I'm annoyed that you picked it instead of *Selling Sunset*.

'They said I was a witch,' I'm saying. I've told you this so many times. You're my oblivious therapist. 'But really I was just a girl born in the wrong era. I'm a twenty-first-century queer girl, in a seventeenth-century body. Not any more of course, though I'm still wearing the clothes I had on the day they –'

You turn. You nearly look at me. You say: 'Shut *up!*'

I've never heard you sound angry, and I have to say, Lily, that for a moment I'm livid right back atcha. All this time I've been wearing down the barrier, and when you do speak to me, it's to be fucking rude.

But then I remember that this is all new to you. That I've been here nearly four hundred years, and you're not even thirty. If I'd lived to thirty, I'd likely have been a closeted grandmother. Things are different now and thank the lord for that. I bite my curses back.

'I'm sorry, darling,' I say. I study your face. You're surprised.

'Did you say sorry?' You whisper it, so gently that I can barely hear the words. But you spoke to me! It's the first time anyone has spoken to me since my own father said: 'This will make you meek.'

'I did, my darling,' I say. 'Don't worry. I'm your friend.'

You sit back for a long time and think about it. After a while I can see that your lips are moving.

'You have to say it out loud,' I say. 'Or I can't hear. Don't worry. There's no one else. Just me and you.'

You breathe a few times, and then you do it.

'Are you...' Your voice is quiet, but it's there. 'Are you a... ghost?'

The word hangs there. It's not a word I've really applied to myself, but I'll take it.

'I am, my darling. I am. I've lived here since long before you were born.'

'How long?'

'Seventeenth century.'

You nod. I watch your face. I wish you could see me, too.

'What's your name?' you say.

'Maggie. Like Maggie Thatcher, but nicer.'

You smile at that. 'How do you know about Maggie Thatcher?'

'Oh, I've kept up with everything. When people used to have papers, I'd read them over their shoulders. Now I look at telly and the internet with you.'

I see you shiver, and I wish I hadn't said that. 'You... you look at things with me? Oh my God I'm so sorry, Maggie. I mean, I only read gossip and I only watch crap!'

'Are you fucking kidding me? I love crap. Can we have *Selling Sunset*?'

You laugh. We talk. When you go to bed that night, you put on episode one of the new series of *Selling Sunset* and leave it playing for me, but I go upstairs and watch you sleeping because even *Selling Sunset* is shit compared to you, Lily.

As soon as you get used to the idea of me, we become friends. You cheer up. I cheer up. I remind you to take your packed lunch. You tell me about work, and when I say it all sounds fine to me, you laugh and say that maybe it's not that bad after all. I put things in perspective for you. That's what you say.

After a few days you say: 'Why are you here, Maggie? I mean, I'm glad you are, but why are you the only one hanging around? What happened to everyone else?'

I sigh. I lie on the floor and stretch out. We've been doing yoga videos and I'm trying to be flexible even though I'm a ghost and it really doesn't make a difference. I do it to practise being like you.

'I wish I knew, my darling,' I say. 'I mean, for hundreds of years I thought it was my punishment. Stuck here forever, seeing the world changing around me but I couldn't do anything. It takes a lot of work even to spook people. I've watched other people die in this house too, and they all just go poof.'

You sit forward on the sofa. You want to work this out.

'Maybe there's something unresolved.' You're excited about this.

'There's nothing unresolved,' I say, and I tell you what happened. I tell you how they killed me. I tell you that my father did it on purpose, to stop me bringing more shame on them. I tell you that my body is buried in this garden, under the apple tree, that no one has ever dug it up. You offer to call the police and get me moved to a proper grave, but I tell you not to bother.

'Maybe your spirit was too strong to go,' you say. I shrug. I've long since given up wondering this: I don't give a shit any more. Still, I like it that you're interested, so I say 'maybe it was!' as if I'd never thought of that before.

You ask me to stop watching you sleeping. 'It's a bit weird,' you say. 'It makes me feel self-conscious.'

I'm hurt. I mean, I could watch you sleeping anyway and you'd never know, but that's not the point. I promise I'll stay downstairs and ask you to leave the TV playing a documentary channel, because then I'll have some facts to tell you in the morning, to keep you interested in me.

And that night's viewing changes everything.

I watch the programme and I spend the rest of the night

wondering, planning. I always hoped this could happen, but now I think I have an idea about how to do it.

In the morning I say, ever so casually: 'I watched a thing about out-of-body experiences. About lucid dreaming.'

You're brushing your teeth. 'Oh yeah?' You spray toothpaste around as you do it. You are living in the golden age of dental hygiene. And you don't even floss! I'd love to experience the sensation of brushing my teeth. I look at the drops of foam on the mirror. You're not going to wipe them off, are you? I'd do it for you if I could. I would floss, if those were my teeth.

'Lily – I think you could do it. Practise and have an out-of-body experience. You could see what it's like to be me.'

You give me that little smile and say: 'Really, though? I mean, it wouldn't work, would it? Not really.'

'Hey, negative Nelly! We could try at the weekend.'

'If you like, Maggie. Sure. Why not?'

You're much more cheerful since we started talking. Much more positive.

We begin on Saturday. Focus. Write down your dreams. Control your dreams. Control your spirit. Dream about leaving your body. Really leave your body.

Slowly, slowly, slowly, it starts to work.

'I can't leave my body, Maggie,' you say. 'That doesn't happen. It's not a thing.'

I give a little cough, and gesture to myself, though you can't see me. 'Er,' I say. 'Hello?'

You laugh. You keep trying. You're so sweet, Lily. So easily led.

I have promised that I don't watch you sleeping any more, but these days I do, particularly when we get to the point in the night where your spirit starts to stir. Usually around three o'clock. Then, I sit on the edge of your bed, watching and waiting.

And it starts to happen.

One night, there you are. A sleeping, breathing Lily, and then another Lily, pulling away from her, looking down at her own self. I gasp. You do too. You look at me and you see me for the first time. Your eyes go wide.

'Maggie?'

You forget to be annoyed that I lied about watching you sleep. You ping back into your own body, but it's a start. I am ready to be very, very, very patient.

We talk about it in the morning. I celebrate you and congratulate you and tell you you're brilliant, and since there's no one else in the world who ever says anything like that, you are encouraged. You try harder and harder. You crave approval and encouragement and love, and I lavish them all upon you.

And, in the end, it pays off.

You're thirty-one now, still working in the Council Tax department at County Hall, and nothing much has changed in your life, apart from the fact that you now have a best friend. A dead woman with an ulterior motive, sure, but a friend nonetheless.

You are good at it now. You do it in your sleep. You go to sleep knowing that at the right point in the night you will leave your body and sit with me, spirits together. You can see me, and we laugh at my funny clothes. Then you ping back to yourself.

'Why don't you leave the room?' I say, one night in March.

'I can't.'

'Try it.'

You give me a wicked little smile. You step towards the door. You are going further from your body than you've ever been before. I can see it trying to pull you back, to suck you back in. Your body is not ready to die: it is hungry for a spirit.

I am closer to it than you are.

I am a spirit.

I'm taking a huge risk because this is the only time I'm going to be able to do this, because if you catch me trying you will move out of this house and it will be over.

You leave the room.

'I'm here!' you say. 'On the landing! Come and see, Maggie! I did it! Look, I'm standing on the bannister!'

I don't come and see because I am lying on top of your body. Your sleeping body, hungry for a spirit. I am on it, and then it starts to pull me in. Things shift. I feel myself changing. I start to feel things that I haven't felt in hundreds of years.

I feel... alive. I think about fingers, and your fingers move.

I can move your fingers.

They are my fingers now.

I had forgotten how it feels to inhabit a body. I had forgotten the magic of existing in a time and a place. Of interacting in a real way with everything around you. I suddenly remember sex.

'Maggie?' you say. You are back in the doorway. Back in the room, but I can't see you now. 'Maggie – where are you?'

I sense you trying to get back in. I hope you won't manage it: both of us in the same body would be a fucking nightmare. I do everything I can to keep you out. I close your eyes, and I fall asleep.

I wake up because the alarm's going off. I check it: seven o'clock.

I go downstairs on wobbly legs and put the kettle on. I make a coffee. I've been practising this for years. I add oat milk. It tastes weird, not at all how I expected.

I pick up the remote and switch on the telly. I switch it on and off lots of times because I can. I make some toast and eat it with butter and jam. Wow! Coffee is worse than I thought but toast is much much better.

I pick up the car key and your lunch and head to work. Turns out driving is literally impossible, so I give up and walk down the track and out of the gate instead. I run to the end of the lane. I breathe the air.

I look around. I exist. I am real again.

I can shut your voice out if I try hard enough. After a couple of days, I type an email to your – my – landlord. Hitting those computer keys with my fingertips is fiddly but I get there.

I am writing to give notice, I type. I make a phone call and arrange to go and look at a flat in Truro, near the station. A flat that I hope does not contain any ghosts. I don't think I'll ever get the hang of driving, so I need to be near the trains.

I leave my cottage for the last time. I hear your voice as I go but I shut it out.

'Maggie!' you yell. I hear you smashing all my stuff.

You'll be OK, Lily. You know what to do when the next person moves in.

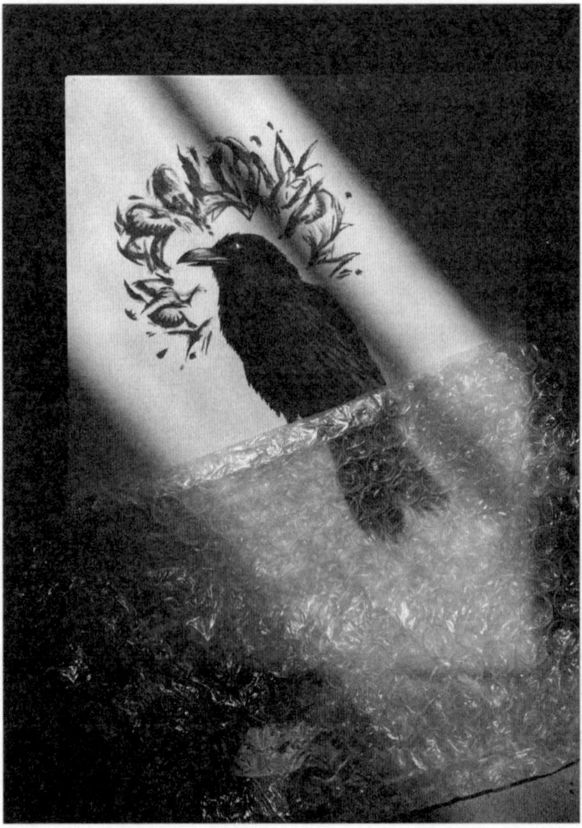

Treloyhan Manor
Nicola K Smith

Annie watched the other passengers as they gazed at the seascape unfolding beyond the train window. The April sunshine flooded the carriage and the sea danced below. At St Ives they tumbled onto the platform, some streaming down the hill towards the town and harbour, others hurrying towards the steps, drawn by the gilded sand.

When the clamour had subsided, she heaved her rucksack and camera bag from the rack and followed in their wake. She had booked the cheapest room she could find, niggled by guilt that she should now be in New York with Ed. Unable to sustain the façade of excitement any longer, she had cancelled the wedding with just two weeks to go. The expectation of happiness had smothered her. She had been barrelled along by others for long enough.

Her own mother had taken the news worse than Ed. Then her in-laws had weighed in. It finally tipped her from shame and self-loathing into a perverse sort of waywardness. She fled to St Ives, synonymous with the freedom and gaiety of her childhood holidays. It was her happy place.

Annie walked towards Carbis Bay, leaving the crowds behind. The afternoon sun was starting to fade, a breeze picking up. As she neared the crest of the hill, she paused at the top of a drive which wound enticingly away from the road and escaped towards the sea. It was flanked with vast trees, their unruly branches forming a dense archway overhead, as if inviting her in. A mass of grey stone could just be glimpsed through the foliage. She picked her way down the broken paving stones of the drive.

The building seemed to edge away from her, the drive leading her further and further towards the cliff top before finally revealing itself. She paused. In front of her stood a large, granite manor house, its bold gable end chimneys reaching into the hazy sky, its dark leaden bay windows staring back at her, unblinking.

She took out her camera, keen to shoot the imposing gothic pile against the backdrop of the glinting sea before the sun faded. As she weaved left and right, framing her shots, she noticed slate tiles missing from the roof, while the central panel of a stained-glass window had been smashed. Edging closer, capturing the refracted burst of colour, she felt the first heavy drop of rain on her forehead.

The wind gusted, gently at first, the sun finally surrendering to the clouds as the droplets began to pelt at Annie's feet, the pitter patter almost spellbinding. She took refuge in the stone doorway just as the light changed, plunging her into the shadows. Perhaps the spring sunshine had been a false harbinger of hope.

The voice made her jump. Annie found herself looking into the cornflower-blue eyes of a woman, her look intent, purposeful, her face framed with silky blonde hair. Her woody, aromatic perfume hung in the air.

'I said you're well off the trodden path.' The woman gestured to the surrounding trees, the top of the drive no longer visible.

'Apologies. I wasn't sure if anyone lived here.'

'You have good instinct.' As she spoke the rain intensified, an earthy damp aroma clinging to the air. She raised her voice: 'Come in, have a look.' Without waiting for an answer, she rounded the side of the building. Annie hurried behind her.

The heavy door slammed shut and a sudden silence engulfed them. The woman led Annie along a short stone corridor to an expansive hallway. An ornate red rug covered the floor, its colours faded, its edges tatty. Discoloured squares of wall stood forgotten, where paintings used to hang.

'It's not what it used to be.' She emitted a short hollow laugh. '*Nothing* is what it used to be.'

Annie followed her, the house's faded glory evident everywhere, each room sitting silently, drained of life. Some oil paintings still hung on walls; their subjects forever troubled. As she moved towards the ornate fireplace, the urgent squawk of a bird funnelled down the broad chimney breast, as if it was travelling at speed. She stopped.

'Bloody ravens. They're a pain.' The woman's accent had a barely perceptible Germanic lilt. 'I thought they'd found somewhere else to terrorise but it seems they're back.'

'Such a beautiful old house. Is it yours?'

She looked directly at Annie and held her gaze. 'No. I just live here. Top floor.' She wandered over to the window, runnels of rain streaming down the glass, obscuring the outdoors and lending a sudden intimacy to their encounter. 'It's awaiting development. I have a stay of execution, for how long, I don't know, but these things, they can take months, years even.'

Annie studied the intricate yellowed cornice high above. 'What a tremendous place to live.'

'Sabine,' she said, without offering her hand. 'I'm an artist so, guess it's a cliché but the space, the quiet, the character – it works for me. And you?' She swivelled to look at Annie, standing too close, her eyes travelling down to the camera in her hand and returning to her face. Annie found herself struggling to look away.

'I'm a photographer. Well, just starting out really.'

Sabine led her up the wide staircase to the top floor, gesturing to the empty rooms as they ascended. Annie's footsteps seemed to echo, even on the thinning stair runner. Sabine paused at the stately hall window, raindrops dripping rhythmically from the lintels. Annie could just make out the moody dark blue of the sea through the spindly pine trees. She thought she glimpsed someone sitting on a rock, looking to the horizon, a hunched figure, still and unmoved by the deluge. When she looked again, she was less sure, the sea fret unfurling over the cliff top and playing tricks with the fading light.

'I can see it needs some love, and some money, but it's just…' Annie's words fell away. The house was so far removed from the suburban semi she had shared with Ed, she felt almost intoxicated by the jarring contrast, the sudden feeling of boundless possibility.

Annie ran her finger along the leaded window. 'It's certainly got more character than the chintzy B&B I'm in tonight.' She peered down the grand staircase, imagining the lives played out there. She felt Sabine's eyes on her.

'How long are you here?'

Annie drew in a deep breath. 'Oh, it's open-ended. A few weeks maybe. I've nothing to rush back for.' She wondered now if she had been too imprudent only booking one night. Ed would certainly have opposed such a lack of contingency. But she'd had a longing to create room for chance, for adventure.

'Listen. I don't know your story but...' Sabine's voice was gentle, melodic, its unexpected inflection compelling. 'The room next door to me, it's vacant.' She looked intently out of the window as she spoke, her tall frame silhouetted against the light. 'If you're looking for a base, you're welcome. The rent, hardly anything, because as you can see,' she gestured helplessly towards the ceiling. 'And I can't say how long before the developers move in. But, well, Treloyhan Manor has a way of enchanting artistic types.'

Hope seemed to seize hold of Annie, almost squeezing the breath from her. Sabine turned to face her; the meaning of her steady gaze unfathomable.

Annie arrived at Treloyhan Manor the next day. The rain had persisted overnight, rivers running down the drive and pooling on the gravel. There was no sign of Sabine when she knocked at the side door. After several attempts, Annie tried the handle and the door eased slowly open over the swollen floor. She shook the water from her hat and slid her rucksack off her back. She called out tentatively as she got to the hallway. Her voice echoed back at her and quickly died.

A door slammed and Annie spun round. Sabine stood behind her, not a foot away. Annie clutched at her chest and laughed.

'Where did you spring from?' She found her heart racing.

'I'll show you in.'

She had only given the room a cursory viewing the day before, but it had everything she needed. A large bay window overlooked the lawn which ran away to a row of pine trees. The sea, almost indistinguishable from the murky sky, lay somewhere in the distance. The room was minimally furnished: a small double bed, a dated en-suite, a cast iron fireplace, and an imposing armoire spanning most of one wall. There was a large space in front of the window, as if a principal piece of furniture had been removed. Above the bed hung a bold painting, awash with colour, at odds with the timeworn décor.

Annie lay down her rucksack and camera bag in the centre of the room and turned to thank Sabine. She was standing a little back from the threshold, her face partly concealed in shadow.

'I'll leave you to unpack, settle. My place is along the corridor, as I showed you.' She paused, gesturing towards the fireplace. 'There's plenty of firewood in the basement.'

Sabine had retreated before she had finished the sentence, closing Annie's door as she went. Annie inhaled her remnant fragrance and stood in front of the window watching as the rainwater drummed on the granite windowsill.

She sat on the bed and took out her camera, flicking through the shots she had taken. The luminous light had been captured perfectly in one image, streaming in shafts through the clouds, almost unearthly, the house looking venerable yet somehow shy. She looked closer. Among the trees at the back was the figure. She enlarged the photo. It was someone bent over, facing the sea, as if intently painting or sketching. Pinching the shot back to normal size, she smiled at the unwitting addition to her photograph.

Through the trees a strange light played on the water, as if the moon and the sun were competing to light the sea. Annie stretched her arms up in the air, exhaled, and allowed herself to feel glad.

She awoke with a start on her first night at Treloyhan. The fire had reduced to embers by the time Annie had turned out the light, but she woke to the crackle of flames just after 2 a.m., the fire ablaze, the walls alive with a trembling glow. She leapt out of bed to check the damper. She had been tired; she must have left it open. She closed it and the flames shrank as they devoured the remaining piece of wood. Despite the lively fire the room remained icy. Pulling the blankets around her chin, she watched as the orange flames became glowing flecks.

Just after 5 a.m., she had been jolted awake by an insistent tapping at the window, as if someone was knocking. She lay still for a moment, reorientating herself. The noise persisted, growing faster, like a drilling against the glass. Finally, she inched the curtain aside. As she did so a large bird swooped away into the breaking dawn, its scream ripping through the air. Its sleek black form dipped low before soaring high and out of sight. Just the metronomic bellowing and hissing of the waves remained. Annie watched as the murky sky absorbed the streak of light over the sea and the day came to life.

She washed and dressed almost noiselessly – it was as if the dense stillness of the house demanded it. Only as she began walking to Hawkes Point did her shoulders start to loosen. At Porthkidney Beach she marvelled at the unending sky as she crouched to capture surfers in the swell, their exhilaration contagious. It was as if each step along the sand was freeing her from her old life, bit by bit.

She didn't light the fire that evening. She climbed between the icy sheets wearing a jumper over her pyjamas, and two pairs of socks. Sleep eluded her, the weighty silence almost deafening. She had not seen Sabine since she arrived. She thought she'd heard the side door heaved open and firmly closed late the night before, but perhaps she had fallen asleep before Sabine had climbed the stairs. Engulfed in silence, she imagined Sabine just down the corridor. When she closed her eyes, it was almost as if she could hear her breathing.

The spring sunshine returned tentatively towards the end of the week, throwing a milky light through the leaded windows, casting shapes across the dusty floors. Having explored St Ives, Annie determined to walk the coast path to Zennor. As she prepared to leave the house, Sabine appeared. She wore a long silk dressing gown, gliding into the dark corridor as Annie gathered her things.

'Making the most of a beautiful morning.' Once again, Sabine stood closer to Annie than was comfortable. Annie could feel the stone wall cold against her back, yet she felt powerless to move. She hauled herself from the trancelike feeling.

'You're welcome to join me?'

A smile played across Sabine's lips. Annie noticed a fleck of red paint on the soft blonde lock of fringe that fell across her forehead. She fought the urge to reach out, to touch it. She looked down at Sabine's long, capable fingers. They too were marked with paint flecks, long dried.

'I'm organising an exhibition. Lots to do. Enjoy your walk.'

'Maybe we can meet up later – for a glass of wine?'

'You know where I am. Knock on my door,' she said over her shoulder, her voice lingering a moment.

A dormant sensation akin to excitement awoke, spiralling from the bottom of Annie's spine to the top. She stepped slowly outside, newly spirited, and stood for a moment, eyes closed in the warm sunshine.

She pushed thoughts of Ed, of her mother, away from her mind. She was more certain than ever that she had done the right thing; 'a brave thing,' her friend had said, with certainty. Annie joined the coast path and strode along to the harbour.

That evening she sat in Sabine's apartment, both either side of the roaring fire. The room grew warm in a way that Annie's never seemed to. She asked Sabine about her exhibition but she answered in vague terms, introducing tangents, diverting into unrelated narratives. She gestured to her easel in the corner of the room, a sheet thrown casually over it. 'That piece is very nearly finished, very nearly. I have high hopes.'

When conversation ceased, Annie could feel Sabine watching her, seemingly feeling no need to fill the silence. The fire snapped and sputtered. Even the house seemed to be listening, waiting. Annie looked around the room, her eyes falling on a large canvas hanging in the centre of the wall. It drew her in as if it was 3D, the dark greens giving her the sensation of entering a forest. More detail seemed to emerge the longer she looked. The skill of the work was immense.

'It's an old one – seven, maybe eight years,' said Sabine. 'I'm not sure if I like it any longer.'

'It's beautiful. It feels like I can almost walk inside it, lose myself...'

Sabine leant towards her, their knees almost touching. Instinctively Annie leant forward too, their faces just inches apart. Sabine's cerise lipstick always seemed to be perfectly applied, highlighting her full mouth. In that moment, Annie wanted to photograph her, to capture that inimitable gleam in Sabine's blue eyes, flecked with orange from the fire, her suggestive mouth, the inherent undercurrent of danger. Self-control eluded her. She reached her finger towards Sabine to trace the outline of her lips but, in that moment, Sabine leaned back laughing and raising her glass to Annie, as if oblivious to her growing need.

The birds woke Annie again the next morning, just as dawn broke. This time it wasn't a single bird but a flock, and instead of rapping at the glass they seemed to be attacking it. Annie lay motionless, listening as small bodies thudded against the glass, the pounding growing louder, more frequent, the curtailed cries of the birds more tortured, more desperate. She pulled the covers tighter around her, fingers clutching the blankets; she was certain the glass was about to shatter.

The assault stopped as quickly as it had started and as the light around her curtains grew more definite, she could hear birdsong. Annie crept across to the window and waited a moment before plucking the curtain back. Against the bold orange sunrise, the large bay window was smeared with blood, repeated scarlet splotches obscuring her view as if multiple small murders had taken place. Annie lunged backwards. A rivulet of blood trickled down the side of the pane and blotted the granite windowsill. It was as if a painter had flung red paint across a glassy canvas.

She found Sabine in the kitchen downstairs.

'Oh, the ravens. They're a pest,' Sabine sighed.

'They've bloodied the windows, I daren't look out on the drive. There must be a pile of dead birds, killed by their own stupidity.'

Sabine laughed. 'Go and look.'

Annie walked slowly around to the front of the house. There was nothing on the gravel. She peered into the overgrown bush beneath. Nothing. She looked up at her window, the sunrise reflecting off the glass, the bloody marks just visible. She couldn't understand how any creature would have survived such a brutal and relentless beating.

'Have you seen them? Are they big enough to be ravens?' asked Annie.

'Yes. They seem to come and go. At the moment, they are everywhere.' Sabine looked at Annie as if challenging her. 'You mind them.'

'It's just a shock to hear them dash themselves against the window. And what a noise. I've never experienced that before.'

'And they say ravens are intelligent. There must be a reason for it.'

'They want my attention,' laughed Annie, studying the curves of Sabine's body through her silk dressing gown as she coasted around the kitchen.

'Yes, they sense a new resident I suppose. Perhaps it is their welcome?'

'I can think of warmer ones.' Annie forced herself to look away but found her attention returning. 'I must wash and dress. Are you around today?'

'Oh, here and there. This exhibition, it's…' She made an unfathomable gesture and stopped suddenly, staring out of the window.

'Is it your paintings, this exhibition?'

Sabine remained standing with her broad back to Annie. She was silent for several moments. 'It is a mix. My work and other artists. It's unique, I suppose.'

'Well, let me know if I can help at all.'

Climbing the stairs back to her room, Annie thought she heard Sabine murmur assent. As she entered, the heavy door of the armoire creaked open. She pushed it shut but it wouldn't catch, and as she looked closely, a large painting at the back of the wardrobe caught her eye, partially concealed in bubble wrap. Curious, Annie eased it out.

She laid it on her bed and, peeling back the plastic, she heard herself gasp. The picture was unmistakable: its hooded black head and intense dark look, the murderous curved beak, half open, yet the body surprisingly slender and lithe. Annie stared. Its beady eyes seemed to lock onto hers.

Yet despite its chilling form, it was beautifully rendered, delicate brushstrokes picking out the light on its sleek feathers, a threatening potency, the brush creating a savage, knowing glint in its eye. Around its head was a haphazard ring of red graffiti, akin to a spattering of blood. Yet it was unfinished. One wing stopped abruptly while only one claw was complete. There was no signature. It was as if it had been abandoned in a hurry.

Annie thought she heard a foot on the stairway. She tugged at the bubble wrap, half covering the front, and pushed it back into the wardrobe. This time the door clicked easily into place. Heart galloping, heat rising up her body, she stood, awaiting a knock at the door. Nothing came.

The weather was closing in once more as Annie returned along the cliff path from Clodgy Point later that afternoon. Battered by the rising wind, she climbed the steps to the coastguard lookout, perched on the gun battery. The handwritten sign on the outside simply said 'dry and bright', while the forecast warned of high winds and heavy rain. Annie poked her head inside. The occupant lowered his binoculars and waved her in. She noticed a sketchpad on the table next to his flask of tea.

'You've caught me out. I'm scribbling in idle moments. It can be a long day otherwise, particularly in this weather.' He stood up slowly. 'I like trying to capture the gannets, diving for their unsuspecting prey.' Annie noticed he rolled his Rs in the Cornish way, lending a warmth to his voice.

'I'm sure it's a good spot for birdwatching.'

'Oh, you get all sorts – different gulls, terns, shearwaters. Couple of years ago, I saw a puffin, just out here.' He pointed to the vast expanse of ocean in front of them.

'Do you see many ravens?' ventured Annie.

'They're growing in number again. Powerful things, quite awe inspiring really.' He laughed. 'I see you're a photographer, do you draw or paint as well?'

'Not really.' The painting of the raven sprung into Annie's mind, its jet-black shiny feathers, the eyes following her. 'I'm staying at Treloyhan Manor, the other side of town. There's an artist living there – very talented; amazing work. Sabine… she exhibits in galleries.'

There was a short silence as the wind rattled the window.

'Oh Treloyhan, I know. I thought that place was empty now. Being developed, isn't it?'

'Due to be, yes. I'm just there short term.' The statement sounded odd out loud.

He looked at her. 'And Sabine you say, the name of this artist?'

Annie nodded.

He looked out to sea for a moment, murmuring. 'Yes, there were a couple of female artists at Treloyhan. Sad story, what happened.' He shook his head. 'I didn't know the other lady was still around. But I only hear rumours and hearsay, no-one tells me anything.'

'I wasn't aware there was anyone else. I don't know her background…'

The man paused, adjusting the notebook, squaring its edge with the table. 'Awful business. The other lady, her friend, Kerensa, she died. Beautiful girl – bright red hair, you know, very striking looking. You couldn't miss her around.'

'That's dreadful. I had no idea.'

'Found her body on the rocks, washed up, like. She often used to sketch down there. I don't think they really know what happened, if you get my drift. Accident or… But like I say, I don't know the full story.'

Annie stared at him.

'There was talk of doing some memorial exhibition in her name but I'm not sure what's happened with that.'

At that moment a huge gust rose off the sea and shook the window, whistling through the gaps and lifting the page of the man's sketchbook.

'I'd better go before this gets worse.' She adjusted her camera bag on her shoulder, thanked him and stepped out into the wind, pulling her collar up and setting off across the clifftop towards the town.

Sweeping cloud became fine mizzle and a low fog unravelled from the sea like a carpet. As Annie neared the house she paused. She could see the figure further along the headland, in the same spot as before. She could just make out a woman sat on a rock, a sketchbook on her lap.

Annie snatched at her camera and lined up the shot, repeatedly pulling back her hair as the wind swept it across her face. But the fog was ever shifting, the light uncertain. Annie squinted at the screen. The resulting image was too indistinct. She slid her camera clumsily back into her bag and made for Treloyhan Manor.

As she tried to summon sleep that night, Annie heard the side door close downstairs. She had already become used to the drag followed by a clunk as it shut tight. Slow but steady footsteps climbed the staircase. Once again, they seemed to pause outside her door. She called out Sabine's name. Only the floorboards creaked in response.

Annie climbed out of bed and inched open the door. She was met with Sabine's blue eyes, somehow still vibrant in the dim glow of the small hall light. Sabine smiled almost beatifically.

'Come for a nightcap. I can't sleep either.' She drifted down the corridor, as if sleepwalking, yet she was fully dressed.

Annie pulled a jumper over her pyjamas, closed her door and followed Sabine into her apartment. There was no fire tonight, the room chilled like her own. Two small lights glowed from opposite corners.

Sabine handed Annie a short, dark drink.

Annie sniffed it. 'Brandy?'

'The perfect nightcap.'

Annie was grateful for the numbness that seemed to flood her veins with the first sip.

Sabine smiled and sat down on the small sofa, patting the space next to her. '*Prost*,' she said, raising her glass aloft. 'Or cheers, I should say.'

She explained that her mother was German, that she had lived in England since she was ten. 'I'll never go back.' She turned to look at Annie, her eyes sliding down to her mouth and resting there.

Annie reached deep to find her words, any words. 'It gets a hold on you. Cornwall. It gets under your skin.' She steeled herself. 'Have you always lived alone here?'

Sabine's smile faded. She looked towards the fire, as if watching imaginary flames.

'I wondered if you would ask, when you would ask, about Kerensa.' Sabine stood up and walked towards the window. The curtains remained open, darkness beyond. 'She was an artist too.'

Annie watched Sabine's back, the shift of her elegant shoulders. Perhaps she would paint, after all. She could imagine the sweep of the acrylic as it committed Sabine to paper, the light brush strokes depicting her silken hair, the line of her cheekbones, the fine detail of her fingers.

'We lived here. Together.' She turned to face Annie. 'She painted in your room – it was her studio.'

Annie swallowed.

'She was an immense talent. She was… too good. But of course, she couldn't see it. She was racked with self-doubt.' Sabine shook her head. 'She would have these… crises of confidence. They were…' She frowned, her face growing almost ugly with the effort. 'They were debilitating, crushing…'

There was a sudden crack of breaking glass, and the potent odour of brandy quickly filled the air. Annie jumped up and began picking up the pieces. Sabine stared at the debris, as if the act had been someone else's doing. Annie expected blood but only brandy dripped from Sabine's fingers.

'How stupid of me.'

'Sit down.' Annie wanted to take her arm, to guide her back onto the sofa but something prevented her. She stood helpless, the broken glass in one hand.

Sabine sat down. 'They found her on the rocks. Her body. Her sketch book, of course.'

Annie sat down. 'I'm sorry. It must have been a terrible shock for you.'

'We'd had a row, the day before. That stupid painting.' Sabine exhaled. 'Kerensa was working on a painting to enter into a competition. A very prestigious competition, the Cass Prize. She was creating this magnificent raven...' She stopped to look at Annie. 'How funny, yes, a raven. It was a beautiful, an incredible rendering. But of course, she didn't think it was good enough. She lost confidence. It was nearly finished. Yet she wanted to throw it away.' Sabine's hands were folded tightly together in her lap now.

Annie leaned closer.

'I took photos of it when she was out. I wanted to submit it. Even unfinished it was... unparalleled. But she found out. She went crazy. The next day...'

Annie drank in Sabine's intoxicating scent, the brandy, feeling suddenly heady. Sabine fell silent.

'It is a marvellous piece of art,' said Annie.

Sabine looked at her.

'I've seen it. I'm sorry. I came across it in the wardrobe.' Annie paused. 'She was very talented.'

They sat for a moment in silence.

'The exhibition I'm curating. It is in Kerensa's memory.'

'Of course. And you will exhibit the raven?'

Sabine laughed. 'That is what has been tormenting me. What would she really want? I just don't know.'

'You must. Sabine, you must.'

She looked at Annie, her fringe falling across her forehead. Annie thought she saw a kind of peace settle somewhere deep inside.

As Annie padded along the corridor to her room later that

night, she noticed that her door stood ajar. The wind still raged outside, great blows shaking the house, forcing its way through ancient cracks, lifting the slate tiles overhead. It's just the wind, she told herself, creeping in, before closing the door behind her.

This time she steeled herself for the ravens at dawn, drawing the curtains slightly and waking to a bruised sky with only a careless brushstroke of white along the horizon. All was quiet. She lay rigid, awaiting the barbarous onslaught. But as the sky lightened, only the symphony of birdsong gathered heart.

Later that morning, Annie eased the painting out from the back of the wardrobe and carried it down to the hall. She carefully unwrapped it and leant it against the wall. She was standing admiring it once more when she felt Sabine's warm breath on her neck, her perfume invading every part of her. She closed her eyes, unwilling to break the spell.

'I'll take it to the gallery in the morning,' said Sabine. 'They must hang it, ready for tomorrow night.' Her voice softened. 'Thank you.'

The words melted something inside Annie. She turned and looked up at Sabine, her face puzzled.

'It seems very clear now. Of course, Kerensa would want it in the exhibition. She would have come to her senses. Thank you for making me see.'

For a moment Annie thought Sabine was going to reach out and take her hand. Annie almost lifted hers in readiness.

'You will come tomorrow evening. To the opening?' Sabine's eyes were imploring.

'I'd love to.'

The pair stood close looking at the artwork, the cavernous

hall lending the piece new energy. As they studied it, the light changed outside, dissipating through the fanlight, sending shadows wandering across the canvas. It was as if the raven was readying itself for flight.

Annie pulled on her brown suede jacket. She hadn't worn it since that last afternoon with Ed when she had broken off the engagement. She could still recall the utter relief that had flooded through her, even as his confounded boyish expression had torn at her heart. She pushed the memory from her mind as she applied her lipstick. It seemed like another life.

As she was descending the stairs she jolted to a halt. The raven was looking up at her, its ebony eyes following her every step. She checked her watch. In her rush, her anxiety, Sabine must have forgotten to take it to the gallery. Annie continued down the stairs, tugging the bubble wrap around the painting, concealing the look of demonic intent. She called a taxi and waited.

There was already a buzz inside the gallery as Annie pulled up outside, a glow emanating amid the fading evening light, its walls awash with colour as people milled around, glass in hand. Annie searched for Sabine through the window but could not pick out her imposing figure, her lustrous hair.

The noise hit her as she entered, the rise and fall of laughter, the chatter of voices. She stood a moment, overwhelmed by the crowd, before a man caught her eye and began to cross the room towards her, smiling.

She returned his smile. 'Is Sabine here?'

He frowned, leaning his ear closer to her mouth.

'Sabine? I've got a painting. It's Kerensa's. Sabine wanted to ensure it was included tonight.'

The man looked from the shrouded painting to Annie and back again. She laid it carefully on the table and began to reveal it. As she peeled off the final layer of plastic, a hush fell over that corner of the room, a quietness rippling through the gallery.

'Wow,' said a voice, amid a sea of murmurs. 'Unmistakably Kerensa's.'

People began to crowd around Annie as they peered at the painting, the noise in the room picking up again, people jostling her, nudging her back. 'Where's Sabine?' she called again, her eyes searching the crowd.

The man picked up the painting, murmuring apologetically to people as he lifted it over their heads and carried it to the back of the gallery. Annie hurried behind.

He lowered the painting against the wall before turning towards Annie.

Over his shoulder, Annie saw a picture of a smiling red-headed woman beaming back at her. The poster advertised a memorial event, in memory of Kerensa Guy. Annie narrowed her eyes. A smaller photo showed her from behind, seated on a rock with her sketchbook, engrossed in her art. Annie shuddered.

He asked if she was OK.

'I've brought this on behalf of Sabine. I thought she'd be here by now. She'd like it featured in the exhibition. Tonight.' Her voice sounded childish, inadequate.

She looked around. A large photo looked back at her from the centre of the room. She was unsure how she had missed it. Sabine looked lighter somehow, more carefree, a wisp of hair lifting slightly in the wind, her skin bronzed from a Cornish summer. Next to her, Kerensa was laughing. Porthminster Beach stretched away behind them.

Annie continued, still transfixed by the photograph. 'The painting's unfinished, but still…'

'Sabine?' he said.

'I'm renting a room along from hers at Treloyhan Manor.' Annie could hear her own voice rising. 'She was unsure at first but… she expressly wanted it included. Is there time to hang it?'

The man's colleague came over, tottering on high heels. 'Wow.' She stared at the raven.

'This lady said… she said that Sabine sent her with it.'

The woman peered at Annie over her glasses. 'Sabine?'

'She's a friend. We're neighbours.'

'She lives at Treloyhan Manor,' said the man.

'Sabine lives next door.' Annie stood wringing her hands.

The woman looked at the man and back to Annie. 'Sabine… died.'

Annie stared at her. 'No. No. Kerensa died.' She laughed. 'But Sabine…'

The lady took Annie's elbow. 'Sabine died a few months later.' She glanced around her. 'Unfortunately – tragically – she took her own life. A broken heart, they say.'

Annie could feel her mouth hanging open, but she seemed unable to remember how to close it. 'Sabine gave this to me,' she insisted. She glanced once more at the photograph, those blue eyes looking back.

The woman placed her hand on Annie's arm. 'Would you like some water, or a cup of tea? Is there anyone with you?'

Annie scarcely remembered getting back to Treloyhan Manor. She vaguely recalled descending the drive to the house in near darkness, her legs almost buckling beneath her weight as she crossed the gravel.

She stood for a moment in the dark corridor, listening. She could hear her own breathing, fast, irregular, as if it were someone else. The walls seemed to sag now, as if in submission, the house no longer expectant.

She lumbered up the gloomy staircase, pausing at the top. A restfulness seemed to emanate from every doorway. She opened the door to her room and clicked the light on. The space seemed even smaller than before. Her rucksack sat crumpled in the corner, the armoire door gaping wide open, as if extending a welcome. Her camera bag lay abandoned on the desk.

She walked along the corridor to Sabine's apartment. The door sat ajar. She pushed at it, without stepping in. Inside it was just as she had seen it last. Several paintings lay stacked against the wall, the easel stood in the corner, the sheet thrown casually over it. The fire was cold.

Annie stepped into the room. She lifted the corner of the sheet, uncovering the easel to reveal an incomplete painting of a woman, smiling as if at the artist, her copper hair threatening to cascade off the page. It was roughly sketched; one rudimentary eye looked back. Only the hair had been painted. Annie drew the sheet back across the easel, as if performing a reverential act.

Next to the sofa, the brandy bottle sat on the small table. She reached out a hand, overcome by a sudden desire to move it, but the bottle stuck fast to a syrupy ring. She closed her eyes and inhaled deeply. The woody aroma had vanished. The air smelt dank, forgotten.

As Annie stood at the top of the drive, shifting the weight of her rucksack, she turned back, staring at the manor house through the trees, its stone façade inscrutable in the moonlight. A bird swept down from above, a draught of air rushing past Annie's ear. It soared down the drive and disappeared, its muted screech carrying across the dark lawns. A raven. Its black form circled over the house before hovering. Annie watched, imagining the barely perceptible movement of its wings. As quickly as it had arrived it was gone, lifted into the night sky and out to sea, as if it had never been.

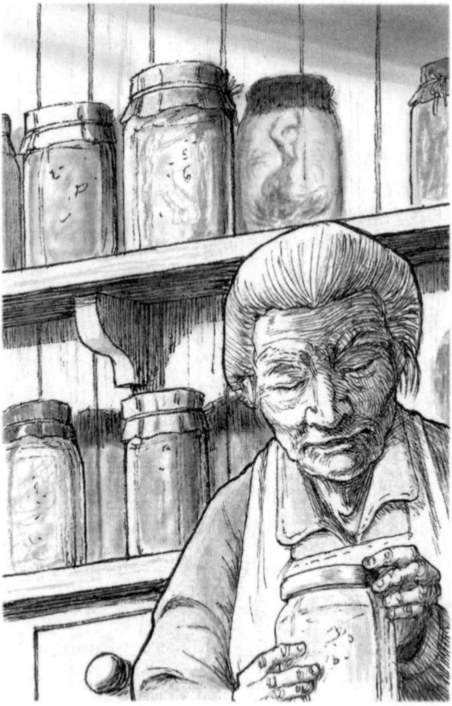

The Visitors

Annamaria Murphy

The sloes lay on the ground, storm blasted, like wrinkled black bullets.

I would risk my life for sloes, and nearly have, the plump juicy ones on the top branch, the ones that as you reach for them the thorns slit your wrists. The stubborn stocky little tree seems to grow as I try to reach that berry and then shrinks back smugly when I give up.

The sloe gin that I intend to make from them, I don't actually like. It's sweet and sickly like cough medicine, but to watch the fruit slowly bleed into the cold, clear liquid, turning it into warm red, is to catch September. But there they lay defeated on the ground in Nanquido Valley, the sound of Georgia's two solitary berries rolling about in her bucket like two lonely tangoers.

The witches had already peed on the blackberries, so that was no good. There was nothing to pick, autumn was coming and there was no escaping it.

Georgia began to sob.

'I've only got two, mummy.'

Then, from behind a bush comes a voice.

'They was all blown off, my dears. If you'd come yesterday, there was fair pickings for all. You come round here with the cheeld, and I'll show you something better.'

So we followed the voice, a cracked voice, with a lilt of bubbling water. A lady old as the mill that no longer turned, or maybe older. Her cardigan caved in, hands conker brown.

'You come in my house a minute. Emeline Trevail,' she said, holding out her hand.

If you go to Nanquidno, there is a house that since a child I have longed to go in. Its shutters are always tight shut like eternal sleepers. It has a twisted tree with a river and a bridge. It's Red Riding Hood, the Billy Goats Gruff, and Hansel and Gretel. And at long last, we were to be invited in.

The door groaned open as she pushed it with her hawthorny arms. The front room was full of rocking chairs, rocking of their own accord, unknown sitters vacated, or maybe the memory of them.

'What you want is Sevilles, my dear,' she said. 'Come in here with me.'

She opened a small door to a pantry. A proper pantry, with cold shelves and a window with a grill. And there the three of us stood, bathed in umber light, bathed in rose and emerald, crimsons and saffrons, golds and lemons. Georgia's creamy-coloured hair was rainbowed, the woman's beige cardigan danced with colours. For each shelf was crowded with bottles packed with liquids – damsons, greengage, sloe, blackberry, elderflower, strawberry liquors, loganberry, limes.

'It's like an autumn sunset off the cliffs there. I come in 'ere sometimes and just stand in it. See this one? I made it the first time I fell in love. Never been opened.'

She took a bottle from the very top shelf. It was marigold orange. She opened it and the smell made us gasp from breath.

She was a girl again.

'Sevilles, that's what you want,' she sighed. 'I was there once you know, Seville. I was a bit of a dancer you know.'

She dances some steps to music in her head, which we too can hear.

'It burns the back of your throat, puts a bit of passion in your veins. Taste that.'

She was right. I tasted emerald and gold and rubies. I tasted Summer, Spring, Autumn, and Winter. She copied out the recipe for me from a book where the ink was fading before our eyes.

'My sister wrote these. She was a dancer too.'

When we left, the rocking chairs still creaked.

A year later, we went back, Georgia clutching a bottle of the precious orange liquid. I hoped Miss Trevail would approve. A farmer looked out from his barn as we passed, his eyes following us.

But the shutters were tight shut and the door bolted. No one at home. We placed the bottle on the doorstep.

The sediment in our bottle rose and danced and settled like a last breath.

We walked away up the track, I asked the farmer if he knew where the old woman was.

'The Trevail sisters?' he said. 'They haven't lived here for twenty years.'

He shook his head.

'Visitors,' he muttered.